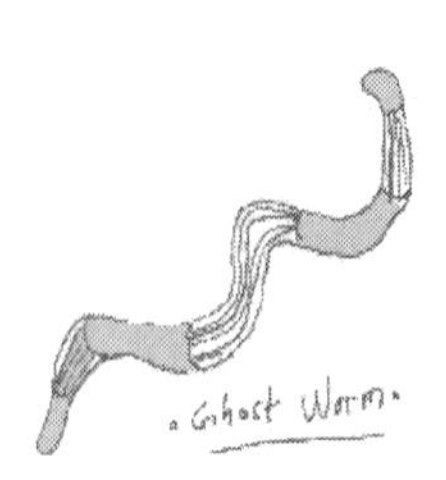

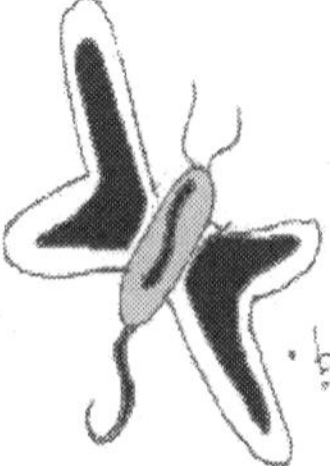

May you
always find
your Meep Sheep ~

Chris Arrr

The Meep Sheep

Chris Ringler

~ Index of the Lands and Peoples ~

(**OR** *Where We Begin and Where We End Up*)

* *Now go and explore this world of dreams and magic and remember to beware the dark.* *

No One and the Bloo Moos

There was nothing to be done, when it came right down to it. No One needed the milk from one of the Bloo Moos near his home if it killed him, which naturally he hoped it would not. Since one of the strange blue cows had already been scared off and was floating several feet up in the air, that left him one option, the cow grazing just down the hill from where he sat. Since Queen Lizzabelle, the third Mistress of Magic of the Kingdom Of Man had fallen from her horse she had fallen gravely ill and was said to be near death. Rumors had begun circulating around the Kingdom and things had gotten so out of hand that the Black Banners that signified the passing of one of the royal family had been brought out of storage in many villages. But while much of the Kingdom was giving up on the Queen, No One wouldn't.

Couldn't.

Just as the Queen was a Mistress of Magic and had a duty she had sworn to uphold, so too had No One sworn an oath he must abide by, and while watching the Great Thicket was the biggest part of that duty, he had also sworn to do all he could to protect whomever held power in the Kingdom, and this was going to be his first real test. The milk of the Bloo Moo, a rare and all but extinct cow in the Kingdom, was known to have healing properties that bordered on the magical and if that didn't heal the Queen, nothing would. So he had to get that milk,

but things were not looking good as on the horizon dark clouds were gathering, as if they too knew the Queen was dying; and should she die and the sun go out for any great length of time there would be an upheaval, something the neighboring Kingdoms (some who still bore grudges after the long wars that had once swept the lands) would love to see happen. No One, planted soundly on his rear after losing his chance to milk the first Bloo Moo nodded to himself as if agreeing to something unsaid.
Whatever happened, however long it might take, he couldn't fail again.

No One picked absently at the weeds as he watched the Bloo Moo chew, chew, chew on the grass that blanketed the hillside, unsure what he should do next. It was clear from the bruise on his bottom that a direct attack wouldn't work, and he didn't risk another one for fear the cow would inflate and take to the sky as its companion had. Bloo Moos had developed a way to escape danger and that was to inflate to many times their size so they could float away to safety, their tails spinning around and around to push them forward. So, if the obvious wasn't the answer, then what was? No One's head ached at the thought of it so he looked up and there, as if mocking him, floated the other Bloo Moo, passing through the clouds and slowly, very slowly coming back to the ground, though it was clear it would be nowhere near where No One was. No One looked from the sky to the ground to where the other cow was grazing listlessly, its tail swishing back and forth and its dark blue spots pulsing with the beating of its twin hearts. As No One watched the cow, a Bumble Kitty buzzed by, its fluffy feet brushing through the long grass and distracting the cow; but instead of inflating, the cow stood dazed as the kitty purred a melody. Bumble Kitties had been said by some to have been the companions of the Song Mothers of old and they could harmonize with someone should they hold the keys of music in their grasp though not many along the lands seemed to be able to do that. Ah, but here, here was a Bumble Kitty, buzzing around on a lazy Spring day and playing with a Bloo Moo, and, it would appear, lulling the cow into a daze with its song. That moment came and passed though and the kitty, apparently bored already and desperate for a nap, flapped its wings (similar to a butterfly's only smaller) and buzzed its way into a nearby tree and fell fast asleep.

A light turned on in No One's head, and behind him there was movement in the Great Thicket, as if in agreement with his idea, which brought a smile to his lips. It would not be the first time the Thicket, the last great mystery left in the Kingdom as far as he knew, had given its feedback to the man, and this time it couldn't have been more helpful.

No One stood slowly, keeping his eyes on the cow, which had come back to its senses, and when it was up he walked over to a basket that sat outside the door to his home. In this basket, which his mother had woven for him when he had left his home to come to the hill to watch over the Great Thicket, was a Sighing Pipe, a gift from his father. He had not played it in a great many weeks but No One would never forget how to call music from the thin piece of willow wood, and that gift was one of the things that made him the Watcher of the Thicket, so he grabbed up the pipe and turned to see that the Bloo Moo was still where he had last seen it.

The cow had its back to him and was a bit further down the hill, but it was still there eating grass and minding its own business. The other cow had finally landed and was off in the distance also eating grass. No One knew he would have one chance to do this, so he bent down and grabbed up a small wooden bucket in his free hand, slipped his shoes off, and began moving slowly down the hill. No One's heart was racing as he walked, and he could feel the sweat running off his bald head and down his face. Each new drip was another distraction but he made himself concentrate. After half an hour passed No One was finally close enough to the Bloo Moo so he put the Sighing Pipe to his lips and began to play. The song that came was soft, and the wind, which had just been blowing through, nearly stole the song away completely, but No One blew harder, closing his eyes as he did. The song was sweet, one his father had taught him, and it had always made him think of sleeping by a gentle pond on a warm day. When he finally opened his eyes, he saw the Bloo Moo's head was up; and its eyes were glassy; and its spots pulsed not in time with its hearts, but with the music.

He had it.

He really had it.

No One began moving down the hill, step by step getting closer to the cow, and he was so close, he almost had it. He got to the cow and sat lightly on the ground and positioned himself so he could milk the cow, which would be none too happy to give it up were it not for the music. Ah, but then came the problem – how could he keep playing the music to keep the cow enthralled *and* milk the cow. It had to be one or the other.

There seemed to be no choice – he had to risk it and stop playing so he could milk the cow.

Oh, and what a mistake that was.

As soon as No One stopped playing the music, the Bloo Moo came to its senses, and looked down at No One, and shook its head angrily back and forth, and then bent down and butted its head gently against No One's, and let out a long moo, and started inflating. No One could only watch helplessly as the cow's dark blue hooves left the ground and

the cow started to hover over the grass. Inch by inch it was rising and as it rose his hopes fell.
He could grab the cow, grab it and forcibly take the milk from it, but that was no way to get it, and he knew it. If the cows were scared badly or angered deeply enough their milk turned sour and could cause the drinker more harm than good. No One's heart sank. He looked down at his bucket, then at his pipe and both seemed useless. The cow was hovering now, six feet in the air, and beginning to look for its friend. No One lifted his arms uselessly and waved them at the Bloo Moo, and his fingers grazed its hooves, which brought its attentions again and brought out another moo.

Just as all seemed lost, the Bumble Kitty No One had seen earlier popped into view overhead, spinning in circles as it lazily flew around the cow, once, twice, three times, and finally landing on the cow's back, which the Bloo Moo did not like in the least. As soon as the cow let out a warning moo the kitty started purring the song it had before, and immediately the cow's head dropped, its eyes became glassy again, and it started to deflate and come back down to the ground. The cow landed exactly where it had just been standing, and when it was down it stood placidly, swaying on the grass in a daze. No One looked up and the kitty looked down at him, its eyes droopy already with sleep as it swished its fluffy calico tail at him as if telling him to get on with it.

No One dropped his Sighing Pipe and placed the bucket beneath the udders of the cow and gently began milking it. Out of the Bloo Moo came magical blue milk which splashed down into the bucket; and within minutes the bucket was full; and as soon as it was, No One looked up to the kitty and nodded to it and it swished its tail in response. The kitty stood on its furry paws and started flapping its small wings and hovered into the sky and off of the cow, ending its song and flying back into the trees for another nap. The cow slowly came to its senses and as it did No One stood and looked at the beautiful creature. His heart ached to know there were so few of them left. The cow turned and looked at No One, then down at its bucket and let out a moo. No One, unsure what to do, leaned forward and laid a hand on the cow to pet it. The Bloo Moo was furry, though the fur was tight to the skin of the cow, and it was softer than anything he'd ever felt before. The cow didn't move away so he stepped closer and rubbed it between its ears, and it closed its eyes and seemed to smile, which brought a smile to No One's face. He rubbed between its ears for a few minutes but was finally stopped when the cow's companion wandered up to No One and mooed. No One looked up and saw that people had noticed the two cows and were coming to see them, or worse, to capture them. The second cow mooed at No One and he nodded and removed his hand, and the cow he had been petting let out a moo and started to inflate. In a moment both cows were hovering and within minutes they were twin blue clouds floating off and away into the sky. The people arrived just in time to see the cows disappear into the clouds, and No One saw from the look of the people and the ropes they had brought, that their intentions had been less than wholesome. The people, angry now and frustrated, looked at No One's bucket, and suddenly he realized he had no way to get the milk to the Queen, and from the look of these people, it might never make it there. Then, just as miraculously as it had appeared before, the Bumble Kitty was suddenly at No One's feet, purring and rubbing itself against his legs to get his attention. It then wandered to the bucket of milk and rubbed against it and looked up at No One, who smiled and nodded.

As the people watched, confused and still angry, No One slipped rope that he used to carry the bucket over the kitty's head and onto its back, and in a moment it was up and hovering, the bucket swaying heavily below its belly, and then slowly it rose higher and higher until it was over the heads of everyone and away towards the high hills and the royal citadel, where the Queen lay. Satisfied he had done all he could, No One bent down and picked up his Sighing Pipe, turned his back on the people and played his way up the hill and into his home. Within an hour the people were gone, probably noticing they were too close to the Great Thicket for comfort, so he took a long nap.

No One woke late in the night to the sound of purring and when he opened his eyes, he saw his furry friend from earlier, the fluff around its mouth dyed a blue that looked suspiciously like the color the milk had been. No One sat up suddenly but before he could get angry a soft hand fell to his shoulder to calm him.

"Your friend here did as it was bidden, dear No One, do not worry. It seems I did not need as much milk as you sent, so I let our friend here have the rest, something he was very happy to have" Queen Lizzabelle was stunning, her long red hair hanging over the shoulders of her pale yellow gown, and she gave off a scent of flowers that made his heart hum. Her eyes were a clear blue that almost glowed in the dim light of No One's home, and he was enthralled by the beauty of the young Queen, but the kitty was there to wake him from his stupor with a bat of its paw.

"Mmm, M'lady, it makes my heart glad to see you back to health. I am so glad it worked."

"Believe me, friend No One, so am I. So is everyone. The clouds were gathering, and we have no time for wars anymore. Not at all."

"But, but why are you here?"

"I was dragged here from my bed by your furry friend, who seems to feel it was appropriate that I thank the man who saved me, and I tend to agree. I thank you both, as well as the cow that gave you its milk, but you, I think, are the one who can pass around my thanks."

The Queen leaned down and kissed No One gently on the forehead, then on each cheek, and finally on the chin, caressing his face as she did, and as she kissed him his body felt as if it was on fire. She pulled away from him and laid a hand on the Bumble Kitty to pet it and then turned to head for the door.

"I must be off, or my counselors will be none too pleased to see I am already out and up to mischief so soon after my recovery. Thank you, friend No One, I truly owe you my life, and the Kingdom owes you a debt it may never repay. Know, though, there will come a day when you will be needed more than ever here as you guard the Great Thicket against the fear and ignorance of a confused world. That day is coming, but not yet, no, not yet, so for now sleep my friend, sleep and rest, and know you are forever in my heart."

And then she was gone. He lay back down and

looked up at the ceiling, lonely but still on fire from her kiss, and his head full of a hundred things that rolled back and forth and back and forth. As if in answer to his loneliness, the kitty looked down at No One, upside down as it stood on the pillows beneath his head, and pushed its furry face down at him so its forehead, touched his. It purred and rubbed its face on No One's forehead and he laughed and awkwardly grabbed the kitty in his arms and held it close as he fell into sweet, sweet dreams.

Messy and the Meep Sheep

Messy dropped her head into her hands and let out a long sigh, her rainbow colored hair hanging down and around and over her face. The village was going on day four hundred and eighty three of the cloud-out that covered the sky in a drab gray and hid the sun from view. The weather had been *so* bad for *so* long that every day the weather person would predict a *strong* chance of sun for the next day, not really certain if that was true or not but wanting to give people some sort of hope, even if it was false. It seemed no one knew what was happening in the Kingdom of Man to take the sunshine away but Messy knew the truth, and knew it all too well - there wasn't going to be any sunshine. Not that day, not the next, not the day after the next, and perhaps not ever again.
The clouds had come over the land and the only person who could do something about that was helpless to do so, and could only watch as people became sadder and sadder. But try as she might, there was nothing this one person could manage to bring back the sun, and it broke her heart.

You see, Messy was an only child, a fact that by itself was not remarkable, but when linked to the fact she was the only child of the greatest Mistress of Magic the Kingdom had ever seen, that made her being an only child quite important indeed. There had been several Mistresses before Anamare,

Messy's mother, and the keepers of the sunshine and the happiness in the Kingdoms of Man, but none had had as much impact on the Kingdom as the current Queen. Save for one, the Mistress of Magic and the Queen were one and the same person, though their responsibilities were never the same, but both had become vital to the Kingdom of Man.

The Queen maintained peace, while the Mistress maintained happiness, and it is the Mistress to which we turn our attention. The duty of the Mistress of Magic was to make sure there were never more than three sunless days in a row; that the crops received the rains they needed; and once a month they would make sure something magnificent happened to bring the people together, friends and family, for one great celebration. For Anamare this monthly event meant she would make certain the winds would blow with cotton candy and caramel corn and that the Carnival King and his roaming carnival would arrive on pink clouds for one night of fun and excitement to help people momentarily forget their problems and troubles.

These monthly celebrations did not solve the many issues people had, but they reminded everyone things were never as dark as they seemed, as long as there was hope.

And this is how it had been for several hundred

years; a hundred for each Mistress…until, that is, Messy's time to rule came. Messy, who had never wanted to be a Mistress of Magic but had wanted to be an Artist and to bring happiness not from the sky but from the heart, was the first to ever turn away from her birthright. She loved and appreciated the things her mother and her grandmothers had done, but she wasn't interested in that life for herself, wanting instead to find her own path and her own way. Something her mother approved of, and nurtured in her daughter. Upon hearing this, the attendants to Anamare were enraged to hear of Messy's wishes - how could she refuse her family duty? How could she turn her back on her people? Word spread among the people of the Royal Citadel, and wherever she went, she was looked upon with angry eyes. And poor little ten-year-old Messy was heartbroken. She left the palace and ran out to the edge of the nearby woods and sat and cried, and cried, and cried until finally she fell asleep, exhausted, and found comfort in her dreams. When she awoke, she found her mother sitting beside her, with Messy's head in her lap as she played with her thick, colorful hair.

"Messy my dear," her mother said. "I would never want you to do something you do not want to do. Our family gladly took on the roles of Mistresses of Magic in the hopes of bringing some sunshine and happiness in a time when there was little of it in the Kingdom, but that doesn't mean, and has never meant, that you were obliged to do as we had. If you have another passion, then follow it."

"But mother, everyone will be mad at me." Messy answered.

"Oh, honey, happiness and hope come from more than just sunshine and the things the Mistresses have brought. If it is Art you love, then you can bring these same things. You can change the world with Art. *You can change the world with Love.* It doesn't matter how you do it, just that you love what you are doing, and that, my dear daughter, will change the world. As long as you believe in yourself, you are never alone. *As long as you believe in yourself there is hope.*"

Messy looked up at her mother and saw nothing but love there and began to cry again, though this time with joy, and she sat up and gave her mother a hug and both of them stayed this way, in each other's arms for quite some time. The last thing she had ever wanted to do was to let her mother down, to let her people down but how could she serve them if she didn't follow her heart?

When word got out Miss Messy was not going to pursue the Arts of Magic, as her mother and grandmother had, but would pursue something else

entirely the people became deeply worried. What would happen if there *was* no Mistress to keep the sunshine in the sky? For years the Kingdom had suffered with darkness, a curse imposed by a Mistress of Menace (who had lived nearly a thousand years earlier) and the Mistresses of Magic had spent their years healing that curse but, should one not be in power, would the curse and darkness return? In fear of this happening, many of the people of the Kingdom wrote Messy letters, begging her to re-think her decision, to take the eight years she had until she was to take over as Mistress and to think about things more carefully. But Messy never got one of these letters; her mother making sure none of them reached her.
Messy had made her decision, and it was hers to make. The people would have to understand that over time and learn to hold hope closer to their hearts. If she betrayed her heart, she betrayed them. She had to trust in herself.

And so the eight years passed, and Messy, day by day, fell deeper and deeper in love with Art, and was happier and happier every day that passed. And so long as Messy promised to work hard at the arts, Anamare promised to make sure the best artists in all the lands came to teach her daughter. And as the years passed Messy developed new styles, new

techniques, and would master new art forms, and once one was mastered, she moved on to the next. Drawing, painting, sculpting, sewing, writing, poetry, all these and more she began to master, and after every finished work Anamare would have the art displayed in the center of the Citadel for the people to see, hoping these works might inspire a sense of wonder and happiness in the beauty.
But they did not.
While the people appreciated the art, seeing the pieces only reminded them that soon, very soon, their Queen would be gone, and they would be left with a new Queen - but no Mistress of Magic.
No one told Queen Anamare of the growing unrest, though it could be said no one needed to tell her, and so the years passed and like all wounds that go untreated, the pain in the Kingdom only deepened with the passing of time.

As grand as her reign had been, Anamare was deeply saddened as the last eight years of her rule came to a close. The people had never really opened their hearts to Messy or to the fact that after Anamare's reign, the sun would only come out when it was ready to, and what she realized, but the people did not, was that the sun only came out when there was enough happiness to push the clouds away, and that was why the sun had gone away in the first place. This was something one of the old Queens had tried to tell her people but which had never been believed so it became necessary to force the clouds apart from time to time, though not nearly as often as the Kingdom may have believed. The people had become so sad so very long ago that a layer of Gloom Clouds had formed and had hung heavy and low ever since. And now, if the people of the Kingdom didn't come out of their unhappiness soon, the sun might never reappear.

But try to as she may want, to get the people to believe in her daughter, there was little she could do for them if they didn't trust in Messy. She had spoken to her advisors, and to people in the community but now it was up to Messy to inspire the sun to rise once more

Knowing what was to come when she was gone, for the last three days of her reign, Anamare let the sun shine all day and all night and asked the Carnival King one last favor – that he would keep the carnival in the Kingdom for those three days. This was how it ended, the reign of Queen Anamare, the Mistress of Magic, and as all the clocks in the land struck midnight on the last day, the Carnival King and all his people gathered to play a regal march as the Queen stepped down from the throne that had been made in her honor by the craftsmen of the kingdom and walked through the rows of the Carnival King's people and the people of the Kingdom of Man. As she passed people were standing shoulder to shoulder and dozens deep to

watch her. The leaving of the Mistresses of Magic was a rare and honored thing, an event people told tales about for decades afterward. Anamare walked slowly through the crowd, her blue dress trailing several feet behind her, and as she passed the people fell in behind, walking mere feet from the train of her dress and all of them silent.
In her hair were fireflies that lit her face up like an angel's, and set a glow about her head. It was the woods she was headed for, a walk of nearly a mile, and everyone followed her the entire way. Everyone took that final walk with her highness - that is, everyone but Messy, who was home doing as her mother had asked, which was to paint a portrait of her mother and the other Mistresses of Magic – who she had described to her daughter in great detail – so they would always be remembered. The portrait would be hung in the castle and would stand as another part of the legacy of the Mistresses.

Messy never saw her mother retreat into the Great Woods, where wonders beyond all imagining lay, and where the Mistresses were all gathered, their laughter lighting the deep, dark trees whose roots ran to the heart of the world, with their happiness. The Mother Wood, it was called, where all gentle souls went when the time of final darkness came. Messy cried as she painted, her own clouds having been over the sun in her heart for a good many years now, and even her Art didn't make her happy anymore.

There was such happiness after the three-day carnival no one seemed to notice that, day-by-day, the sun was dimming, until finally it went out completely, after ten days, and the clouds returned. And thus began the reign of Queen Messy, the fourth Mistress of Magic, who had given up her place among her ancestors in the hopes of pursuing the Arts. Her heart broke, when the sun went out but there was nothing she could do to stop it, forced to watch it dim - just as her people watched - until the darkness finally hid her tears from even herself.

She had hoped that perhaps, just perhaps, the magic her mother had woven over the lands would last, would inspire happiness in the people that would last and push the clouds away but no, the sun was dim, and so were the people.

Darkness had returned.

Day by day the people of the Kingdom gathered at the gates of the castle to plead, beg, and demand Messy take up the magic of her family and bring back the sun. Messy's council, the people who guided the Mistress through much of her reign, did their best to calm the people but were unable to get them to leave; and try as they might, they could not keep the unrest from the Queen. The trouble was even if she had wanted to, Messy couldn't bring back the sun. She had never learned to use her craft, her power, and while it may still be in her, it was so deep that she knew not how to reach it, or to develop it. Deeply saddened by the pleadings of the people, Messy turned to her teachers and asked them if she might still learn how to wield the power, begging them to help her learn the craft of her mother and grandmothers.

"But it's too late, Queen Messy, too late you see, too late."

"But why?" She asked, between sobs.

"Your passions lay with the Arts now, and were you to take up magic and the great crafts, you would create not works both great and beautiful, but works that were sorrowful and sad, as your heart would not truly be in them. You have chosen your path, Mistress, and now it is for you to decide how exactly you can serve the world with that gift."

Messy was eighteen now and stunning, her hair long and thick and looking as if a dozen rainbows had been captured upon her head. She was beautiful even in her sadness, and, after years of putting aside the concerns of the Kingdom, she was ready to face the decision she had made. She hugged her teacher, Mr. Naysmith, who had watched over her since she was a baby, and turned and went to her room, where she stayed for several weeks.

Some way, somehow she had to find a way to bend her Arts so that they could benefit her people and the world as a whole

She had to find a way.

In those weeks she completed the portraits of the Mistresses with such skill and technique as to make all the teachers of the castle (and all those that worked there and set an eye to them) to weep. To look upon the portraits of the former Mistresses of Magic made one feel as if you were looking upon the very person as they stood before you and while the viewer wept, it was with happiness, and not sorrow, and for Messy, this was a start. Each painting was hung in a special gallery, where other works of art created by Messy were displayed, and each was released weeks apart from one another so people could come and lay eyes to them.

One would have thought, judging by the reactions of the people of the Kingdom to see these portraits, that the sun might shine bright again. They were so delighted to see the Mistresses of old, but as happy as the people were to see the art, their joy was fleeting and they returned to their gloom when they left. All but a few of the elders were seeing what the

first two Mistresses looked like for the first time, but sadly, upon seeing the pictures, the depression only deepened. Seeing the former keepers of sunshine and happiness only made the people mourn their passing all the more and deepened their bitterness towards Messy. And so outside the palace the crowds grew and so too did the worry of those within it. But for Messy, who was deep within her arts, lost in them and to the world outside of her room, nothing had changed, nor would it until she found what she was looking for. She felt, deep down, that her people were unhappy, but she pushed those thoughts away, knowing that there was a way to make them happy, if only she could but find the way.
And so things went.

And time passed for the Kingdom and the clouds came low enough that on some days the people didn't know where the ground ended and the sky began. Or if there even was a sky anymore.

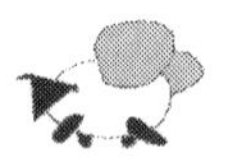

Just as all hope had faded, Queen Messy came out of her seclusion, a woman renewed. After four hundred and eighty two days, she was ready to leave the palace, against the wishes of the dozen teachers who watched over her, but she *was* the Queen so they reluctantly opened the emerald gates that were all but forgotten in the back of the castle and let her out through a secret passage, so she could avoid the people waiting outside the main gates. And for the first time during her reign, Messy saw her kingdom. At first she was delighted, as she ran out into the open air, her boots thumping along the cobblestone path that lead towards the woods, and her smile alone was almost enough to light the sun by itself.

She was delighted to taste the open air, to see the trees, the grass, the ducks, the Bumble Kitties, the giraffes, the Kumberboos and even the hippos that wandered freely across the lands and waded in its waters. It had been so long since Messy had been able to walk freely and she was so shocked and happy to be outside again - a young woman in love with her Art and the world. She looked up to the sky, expecting to be greeted by the sun and its own great smile. But when she looked up she was horrified by what she saw and stopped moving, her body having been in mid-dance, and her smile melted into a frown and her body withered like a flower. She swayed a moment, and then fell onto her knees in the thick grasses nearest to the woods. She'd forgotten, there was no sun.

Not anymore.

And she didn't cry, not this time, instead she just knelt there and looked up into the sky and into the thick gray clouds and was lost there for a time. When she didn't return for lunch, her teachers became worried; when she didn't return for supper they became fearful; and when the clock struck ten, and she was still not back, they set out with torches and sheep – great animals for sensing strong magics – and searched the land for Messy, hoping against hope she'd be found safe.

And she was.

They found her. The three tracking sheep huddled around her and were nosing at her boots. Her head was no longer in her hands but looking out over the meadows as she petted one of the sheep, a distant smile on her face. Mr. Naysmith finally approached her.

"Mistress Messy, are, are you well? We were worried sick when you didn't return. What ever have you been up to?"

And Messy smiled to her teacher and stood up as she answered.

"There's no time for that now Mr. Naysmith I have a lot of work to do. Come on, it's late, let's get back."

And so, with Messy in the lead and the sheep following silently behind her, the teachers made their way back to the castle, heads bowed together as they whispered about what had come over the Mistress though Mr. Naysmith, the last in the group, had someone looked closely, was smiling in the same manner as Messy, as if he somehow shared her secret.

When the party returned, Messy retired to her room and locked the door without a word, which was not peculiar, if she was in one of her moods, and Art was on her mind, but in this instance she had brought the three sheep into the room with her, which seemed quite odd to her council and teachers. Many strange things were heard as everyone – all save Mr. Naysmith – huddled around Messy's door, curious what she was up to, but nothing could be gathered except that it was odd business indeed. And so it was, and so it went, and within, the people waited, and without the people gathered, and the rest was just a mystery.

And far away from prying eyes, Messy was working on a notion, a faint idea that had struck her as she sat out under that starless sky and had been deep in thought. She had been suddenly nudged by one of the sheep, and seeing the black little face surrounded by the cloud of fluff looking up at her, she couldn't help but smile and giggle. And that's when it hit her, the idea that had struck her like lightning and had given her a wild notion that set her mind to motion. And now here she was, in the wee hours of the night, surrounded by dozens of failed attempts to capture the vision she'd had in her head.

What she had seen as she looked down at the sweet face of the sheep was the image of a small sheep, flying through the air on bumblebee wings, flying down and landing beside a frowning child and then something happened between the child and flying sheep, and the child smiled, and above the two the clouds broke open; and there it was, the face of the sun, shining down again for all to see.
But how did she get from that vision to something real?

She wrote a story and nothing happened.
She wrote a poem and nothing happened.
She wrote a song and nothing happened.
She molded clay and nothing happened.
She built a statue and nothing happened.

She drew a picture and felt a brief glimmer of something. Like a shock that ran through her fingers as she finished the drawing. But it wasn't right.

She began to paint, and as she painted, she lost track of time and place and of everything but the painting, and in her heart echoed her mother's words - *You can change the world with art. You can change the world with love.* And she could. *She would.* She could feel that in her hands, in her heart, as she painted with all she had. And when she had finished, the three sheep long asleep and huddled around her feet. Her hands and face covered in paint, she stepped back from the painting and looked at it.

It took her breath away.

Not once had she ever thought she had anything in her like her mother or grandmothers or any of the other Mistresses of Magic yet here, before her, was a painting that, even looking upon it now, made her smile like it was her birthday.

The painting depicted a hill of thick, green grass, and upon it was a child who looked to be the saddest thing in the world yet, at the corners of the little boy's mouth was the beginnings of a smile, a smile that seemed to be in direct relation to the fluffy cloud of cotton that hovered on thin wings beside him. He had one arm flung around the flying sheep, squeezing it, and there above, pushing through the clouds was the sun, breaking the long spell of darkness that had covered the Kingdom for so long.
This was it.
This was really it.

Finally, after hours of seclusion Messy

unlocked her doors and ran from her chambers, to summon her teachers and counselors to see what she had created. It was very late, or very early, depending on your view, and they had all been asleep but came, though warily, to see what she was so excited about. And on seeing the painting, several of them burst into tears, and some others burst into laughter, and yet, Mr. Naysmith was unmoved.
Messy frowned.

"This is it Mr. Naysmith. This is what shall bring happiness to the Kingdom again. This is my Art. This is my gift. It proves I am a true Mistress of Magic. I was so lost, for so long, afraid I would never find a way to bring back the happiness that the Kingdom had lost but now, now I have found it. I really found it. Don't you approve?"

"Oh, dear Mistress Messy, of your talent I can do nothing but marvel at its grace and skill. It is a beautiful picture. I don't doubt many will be thrilled when it is displayed in the gallery."

"But…" Asked Messy, her smile falling.

"But nothing, Mistress, you see, this is not a finished piece."

"What do you mean Mr. Naysmith? How can you say that?"

"Because, Mistress Messy, were it finished, we would see either a little boy, or a hill, or a flying sheep in your chambers, as alive as you or I. You are a child of Magic and the craft, and as such, you cannot help but to *create* magic…when you wish it. As of yet, you haven't reached a point where it is possible, but finally, finally I see you are ready."

"But, but ready for what Mr. Naysmith?" She asked.

"Why, ready to bring back the sunshine Mistress Messy. Now, grab the painting, put your boots on, and follow me."

Messy, more than slightly confused, did as she was asked and followed her teacher down through the castle and out the front gates, the teachers and sheep in tow. At the gates there still stood over a hundred sleepy people, and on seeing the procession exiting the castle, and catching glimpse of the lovely Mistress Messy for the first time in years, the group of them followed along as well, silent and in the spell of the moment. After a fair walk, Mr. Naysmith finally came to a stop atop the highest hill in all the land, a mile from the royal citadel. As soon as they had all stopped, the sheep plopped down onto the grass and began to sleep again, but while they slept, Messy and the rest of the group waited for what Mr. Naysmith would do next.

"Now, Messy, you have painted a stunning picture, and one that has moved me, and all of us who have seen it, very deeply, but while it is art, it is not *Art*. Not *the* Art. Do you understand yet?"

"I think I do. I understand the sun still isn't shining, and people aren't as joyful as I expected. But, but what can *I* do to change that?"

"You can breathe life into it, my dear. With but a kiss upon the thing in the painting you wish to bring into our world, you can do it. Only with your love, your kiss, your *hope* will this be made real."

Messy opened her mouth to speak but then closed it. She finally understood. Maybe she had had the power all along, as her mother had known, but had never really been able to see past her own sadness and worry to see her own magic. She *was* like the other Mistresses, she *could* bring happiness to the land, could return it to sunshine again, but she would do it not with Magic as the others had but with Art, and Love.

Messy raised the picture up to her face and looked at it and smiled. She leaned forward and kissed the flying sheep gently, and as she did she felt butterflies in her belly and a tingling in her toes and many said they saw a spark as her lips touched the canvas. And after she had kissed the painting, she laid it on the dewy grass and stepped away. The crowd of people was silent in anticipation.

At first nothing happened, and one or two people tried to shout something mean at the Mistress but were quickly hushed. Then, as the group watched, the painting moved a little, then a little more, and then yet more, wiggling across the grassy hill as if it were alive. The moving of the painting must have awakened the sleeping sheep because they got up and wandered over towards the painting, their noses sniffing the air as if smelling something the others could not. Just as the sheep were about to reach the painting something furry and white erupted from it and into the air.

The crowd gasped.

Messy stepped back, the tingling now up to her knees. Something whirled and spun high above the crowd, dipping in and out of the clouds as they all watched, until it finally made its way down to them again. As it came closer they could all hear the faint sound of wings and thought the thing was white with a black face but were uncertain. Messy watched as the white shape came closer and closer and closer until she was able to slowly make out details.

It was shaped like a cloud, thick and fluffy, but had a black triangular head with bright blue eyes, and upon its back were thin, rounded wings were like a bumblebee's. It was smaller than a sheep, about half its size, but it *was* a sheep, *her* sheep, the one from the painting; and she smiled as it finally came back to the ground and settled beside her. It came up only to her knees and as it landed it waddled towards her.

The three real sheep, shocked at what they were seeing, moved back behind some of the crowd and looked out from behind the human legs. The little winged sheep finally reached Messy, and when it did, it nudged her on the leg with its head. She shook her head, uncertain what it wanted, and continued to look down at it, but then it did it again, and again, and again.

Baffled, she looked to Mr. Naysmith, who just smiled at her. She finally knelt down to pet the sheep, but as she was going to do it, the sheep slid beneath her hand and up under it into the crook of her arm. Finally realizing what it wanted, Messy squeezed the sheep and it let out a short, "*MEEP*" and Messy couldn't help but laugh. She squeezed it again and had the same results, and the same upon the third and fourth times. And upon the fifth time laughter had spread throughout the crowd, and as they laughed, the Meep Sheep moved amongst them and each one gave it a squeeze and smiled afterward, barely able to contain themselves.

And there, above, as they laughed and squeezed the little Meep Sheep, something happened that had not happened in a *very* long time - The clouds broke, and the sun appeared. And as soon as the sun was out the Meep Sheep took to its wings and was up in the air again and flew in circles around the people before settling upon a far hill to graze, the other three sheep happily chasing after it to make its acquaintance.

The crowd cheered.

Messy was laughing so hard she began to cry. And Mr. Naysmith put an arm around her and gave her a hug.

"Your mother knew you had it in you, all along. As did I. It was just a matter of *you* realizing you it yourself, and now you have. Hope, Messy, and believing in yourself are the most important things a person can have. If you don't believe in yourself, nothing is possible, but if you do, ah, then anything is possible."

"Yes, I, I guess so. I guess I am like the others, just in my own way. But, but what now?"

"Well, you might make some friends for your little Meep Sheep there, that might be in order"

"And beyond that, Mr. Naysmith?"

"Beyond that? Well Messy, you have at least a hundred years to decide that, so I am sure you'll think of something, though I might recommend you see what the Kingdom needs from you and start there."

Messy smiled and punched her teacher softly in the arm, and she and Mr. Naysmith began laughing and then hugged one another, and the crowd came and encircled them, and each one knelt before Messy, the Mistress of Art *and* Magic, and kissed her hand in thanks.

And so it was that sunshine came back to the Kingdom of Man. And as for the Meep Sheep, they began appearing, one by one, upon hills and on meadows and in the sky across the lands as the days passed. Whenever someone was sad or unhappy a Meep Sheep would come to their aid, nudging them until they were squeezed, and upon hearing their familiar '*Meep*' the person would smile and remember what it felt like to have the sun in their hearts again. And yes, the clouds did return, from time to time as clouds often do, as even Mr. Sun needs a nap from time to time, but the sun was never gone for long, and the people were never very upset when it did disappear, trusting it would appear again when the time was right. And as for Messy, well, she found happiness, in not just her Art, but in herself, and that was her greatest gift of all. And for her, the adventure had just begun.

Ashley Pickles and the Bumble Kitties

Music was everywhere.
Wherever he looked, wherever he was, and whatever he did, music was there, waiting for him like a friend. It was there and had been there since a good friend had taught him how to find it in everything.
It was there...until it was gone.
Until suddenly, awfully, it was gone.

It had been three weeks since someone else had taken the spotlight Ashley Pickles had known for so long, the very place where he had gained the love and attention of the people, but worse than that, it had been days since he'd been able to sing. Ashley was worried.
He was scared.
Ever since he was a boy he'd had the gift of song and the magic of music but suddenly, it was gone, as if it'd never been there in the first place. Ashley hung his head and looked down at the green grass of the Kingdom of Man and felt sorry for himself. It had been a month since Queen Messy had returned the sun to the people and the word of her feat, and of the wonderful creatures her magic had spawned were still on the lips of everyone. Ashley had yet to see one of her Meep Sheep that were said to bring sunshine to the heart, if not the sky, but he knew their work well and had it in mind to write a song in their and Mistress Messy's honor, though he hadn't gotten to it just yet. He'd gotten distracted, which

happened a lot these days but never before had he reached a sort of creative dead end, where he wasn't able to think of a song, *any* song to sing.

Something was different.

Maybe *he* was different.

It had been days since the songs had left him, and since he had stopped hearing the music in his heart and he was getting not just worried but scared. All of the music that he heard every moment of every day and in every thing he saw was gone. All that remained now was deafening silence. He couldn't write a song, and couldn't even remember or sing the songs he'd been singing all these years. It was all gone. It was almost as if when sunshine came back to people's hearts, he stopped being able to sing songs.

What if he'd lost his music?

Ashley sighed and ran his hands over the knees of his worn corduroy pants as he listened to the sound of the wind in the grass and wondered what to do next. He closed his eyes, opened his mouth and let his heart speak but the only sound that came out was a belch that was a result of too much lunch an hour earlier. Ashley – Ash to his close friends – let out a sigh and stood up. It was time to put feet to grass and to get moving. It was obvious nothing was going to happen here. Not today, anyway. He had been under his favorite tree, near his favorite lake, had eaten his favorite meal,

and was even wearing his favorite clothes, but still there came no song from his mouth and no music from his guitar. Maybe it was the place. Maybe he'd been sitting here, sleeping here too long, too often, and needed a change of pace?
Or was it something else?
What was wrong with him?
Was he ill?
Had he used up his gift?
Was it something in the air? The water? The food?
He put a hand to his head and felt no fever. He stuck out his tongue and saw no sickness, though he could not really see his tongue well at all, to be honest. He coughed. He tried to sneeze.
No, he wasn't ill.
What was it then?

He frowned and sighed again, kicking an acorn into the water and sending out ripples that woke the Water-Dragons from their naps and sent them down to the depths in a flurry. *Where were* ***his*** *Meep Sheep*, wondered Ash. If they were so great and all, and brought happiness to people then where were his? Ashley walked to the water's edge and looked into its murkiness for the answer and above him the clouds parted and the sun appeared for the first time in two days, seeming almost to mock his misery. Ashley walked back to the tree, bundled up his lunch and bent down to absently pet the sleeping Bumble Kitty that purred quietly near where he had been sitting. As soon as he touched it the kitty purred deeply and stretched its back to give him more to pet. This was a calico, and had taken to following Ashley around whenever he came to this spot, always begging for attention and pulling Ash's mind away from his music whenever he got frustrated trying to think of a song to sing. He stood back up, to the dismay of the kitty, and started back toward his home. He wasn't ten feet before he heard a familiar meowing coming from over his shoulder and turned to see the Bumble Kitty was following him, it's wings, so very like a butterfly's, beating hard to keep up but unable. Its wings never seemed able to hold up the big, furry bodies, and their short, stubby legs were rarely able to move them very quickly so it was not often that a Bumble Kitty was able to do much more than waddle around, hover, or sleep, their laziness halting them from doing much of anything. Ashley felt bad in leaving the kitty and its bumbling (the sound of its purring intensified by flying), made him want to slow, to stop, and to give it a pat on the head. He pushed forward though and the kitty kept coming. Ashley paused a couple times to see where the kitty was and saw it trailing further and further behind but was finally able to get up enough speed so that it gave up the chase and let out an angry yowl before dropping back onto the grass. This had happened to him before, and not just with this kitty, but with all Bumble Kitties he met. It was funny at first, having so many of the kitties purring and flying around him, but it was distracting and made it awfully hard to get any song writing done. Fact was, whenever he got close to a breakthrough one of the kitties would start to purr and break his concentration. And as he was walking he had a thought he'd had a thousand times before – *I shouldn't go to the tree near the lake anymore.* The tree was a Bumble Kitty tree, a place where they nested and slept, and where many of them usually were. They slept in colonies and you could tell a Bumble Tree as soon as you heard the loud purring that came from it. Ashley had come upon these trees many times and he could never shake the fog that settled over his mind each time he came near so many of the kitties. He became suddenly sleepy and no matter how hard he fought he could never manage to keep his eyes open and ended up asleep under the Bumble Tree in no time at all, spending countless hours surrounded by the purring, pawing, affectionate kitties. But for now, he had lost his companion and was able to avoid the Bumble Trees and the Bumble Kitties completely, and his mind fell back to music.

Music.

The walk back to his small cottage was a long one but Ashley didn't usually mind. It gave him a chance to watch the world and to see all the people and to remember what it was like to bring joy to others. Off in the distant sky he thought he saw something moving slowly and wondered if that could be one of Queen Messy's Meep Sheep but couldn't be sure. He frowned a little at its sight. He didn't know why but he felt bitter and sad, and utterly useless. It was like, now that he couldn't sing, couldn't play, he wasn't important anymore. He didn't matter.

Music was all he had, and, now having lost that, what was there left?

He was born for music as it was born for him. Without the music, what did he have to offer?

No one had ever talked to *just* Ash. No one really bothered with how *Ash* felt. Ashley Pickles though, well, he was someone that people wanted to see, wanted to spend time with, wanted to listen to. Ashley, *that* Ashley was somebody. But now what?

The sky darkened, the trees began to whisper, and Ashley dreamed while he walked.

Every story has a beginning. Even Ashley Pickles'.

Ashley Pickles was born into a good, modest family that lived in the Dark Lands of the Kingdoms of Man, the lands where there was little sun, there was no laughter, and there was little to no music. Ashley's father was in charge of the Department of Shoes and Socks, where he made sure that every person - man, woman, and child - had shoes and socks to wear and were always wearing them. There were few places where bared feet were allowed, due to the Archduke's fear of people stepping on tacks or pins, and so it was Ashley's dad's job to make sure that no one was caught without their shoes. It was a boring job but, as long as the Archduke was in power in the Dark Lands, it was dependable work. Ashley's mother was a Flower Maiden, which meant she was someone who tended to the one garden that lay in the Dark Lands and made sure that the Moon-Stone flowers blossomed regularly and that their clear blue nectar was collected for the magic makers to do their work. The Dark Lands were named such because of how little light was seen and, because of that, no flowers really grew in the area save for the Moon-Stone flower, and a few others which needed little light. It was not the sort of place any child would choose to grow up - the weather was cold and stormy, the children few, and the moods of the people grim, but Ashley seemed to take to the place. Both his mother and father had dreamed of a day when they might get the money together to move away, to one of the other lands in the Kingdom of Man but that day had yet to arrive so they made the best of it and it was a blessing that Ashley became so fond of his home and seemed to find happiness there, as it made it easier for his parents to find their own joys and happiness as well. Where other children moped and complained, Ashley always seemed to be laughing. It was, in fact, during the sixth day of a rain storm that the boy first began singing for the family. The song was a sad lullaby about the old wars that his mother had sung to him when he was still a baby and as he sang his voice was such that his mother and father didn't seem to hear the words at all but were within the song itself.

His voice was a gift.

His voice was magic.

They knew even then that his voice was something different, something special, and it was no time at all until the three year old was being sought out to sing for the family's friends and neighbors. And while they were reluctant at first, his parent's allowed him to go to sing because it made him so happy to make others happy, and there was just so little joy to go around those days.

Ashley's fame had been sudden and shocking to both his mother and his father, though to him, it seemed to come as no surprise at all. He sang that was all, and it was just more fun for him if people were there to hear him, and the more people the merrier. The songs he sang were other people's songs, songs known and loved for years and years and he would put his own life and magic into them, making people sometimes forget the original version altogether. His mother was shocked, she'd told her husband, that all of the songs he sang were sad, and, if someone else were to sing them, would indeed bring tears, and not the laughter that came from a fond memory of a lost one, not the heartbreak of that loss, that was what Ashley brought out – the joy in sorrow. Strange, she'd say, strange indeed. If you were to ask Ashley why he sang those songs he'd simply laugh and tell you that he sang them because they were just the best songs to sing, that was all. It was just that simple for him.

The weeks passed, the months passed, and the years passed and as Ashley grew, so did his gift and his song book. He had yet to write his own song but the songs he sang were so beloved that it seemed not to matter. People didn't care what he sang, just that he sang for them. During this time the family was offered riches beyond belief – jewels, money, houses, and more if only they'd let their son take up singing full time, and let him tour across the Kingdom under the watchful eyes of these managers. Some even said that the power of his song was such that he might even make the rest of the lands forget their troubles like he had done in the Dark Lands. He had become a phenomenon. His parents though never treated Ashley any differently than they had before. He was their son and they loved him, and that was that. He had a gift, yes, and they encouraged him to share it, but they never let him take gifts or money for the gift. No, his father had told him once, his was a gift to share, but, there was a way to make a living from it, if he'd but find it when the time was right.

Ash's parents also knew well enough that the people interested in 'sharing' his talent wanted only to profit from it themselves, that was all. So the family, though offered fame and fortune, remained in the Dark Lands, his father remained in the Department of Shoes and Socks and his mother remained as Flower Maiden to the land, and they were happy. So long as they had one another, the rest would work itself out.
While he had a great talent for singing, it was always without accompaniment, but all that changed when someone entered his life that would change him forever.

Ashley learned to play the guitar when he was ten, when the elderly Archduke took it upon himself to teach the boy how to hone his voice with music. The Archduke, known across the Dark Lands as a cruel, cold man, had heard tales of young Ashley Pickles and his magical voice and had doubted that such a talent could exist. He had heard before of people with talents that might interest him but all of them had fallen short of his hopes. He was a man that had learned to accept disappointment and it wasn't often that something impressed him enough to care but this boy, this Ashley was different. He had heard too many things about him to just ignore what was said. He had to see for himself. One day, while the boy was out singing for some old washer women the Archduke had disguised himself and gone to hear the boy. The old man watched from behind some trees and was stunned to hear young Ash. As Ashley sang the Archduke remembered a time in his youth when he wasn't so focused on power, on ruling, and on controlling people. He remembered a time when all he had wanted was to show the world love and beauty and to bring light to the Dark Lands where he had lived and ruled for so long. There was a time, many years ago, when the Archduke had been a young man like Ashley, and he had wanted to bring happiness through his ability with a guitar but, being born of royal lineage, he wasn't allowed to pursue such dreams and so he let them die. It was a cruel trick of the mountains that surrounded the Dark Lands that they halted much of the sunlight from reaching the homes in the valley, creating an oppressive, sad place to live and raise a family, and it was this sullenness that took root in and grew in the boy that became the man that now watched young Ashley play. The Archduke caught a shiver suddenly as he remembered that boy he'd once been, lost now, and the man he had become - bitter, sad, and lonely.

It was a long walk back to the Archduke's modest castle, which lay beneath the great Elder Trees that rose thousands of feet into the air and which housed many colonies of the Bumble Kitties that made this land their home. He sat up that entire night, deep in thought, and when the gray light of day dawned he sent for the boy Ashley Pickles in the hopes of perhaps doing for him what no one had done for the Archduke. Perhaps he could help keep the boy on the right path, and away from the dark woods he himself had been lost in as a child. It was this meeting, early in the morning, in the grand music room, where the Archduke said the words that changed Ashley forever – *You are here, not so I can teach you to be great, but so I can teach you how to be special. Will you accept that?* Ashley was silent a moment, looking down at his knees and hands, anything to avoid looking at the Archduke, who, fat from his many years of power, was someone the boy had been raised to hate. He had been told, briefly, why he was being summoned, but he still wasn't sure why the Archduke was so interested in him. His parents were worried when he'd been sent for but didn't see what offensive thing their son might have done so they agreed to let him go, though reluctantly. Ash held onto the silence as long as he could then looked up, knowing in his heart that the answer was 'no' He had nothing to learn from this bitter man, nothing but how to hurt and sadden people but just as he looked up into the man's eyes his answer surprised even himself – yes, he replied. Yes.

Now it could be said that his reasoning was self serving but guitar was what the Archduke felt would best compliment the boy's raw voice and once he picked one up, Ashley was a natural. With much practice and under the watchful eye of the

Archduke it wasn't long before he became as good as his master, much to his parents' concern, and to the Archduke's amusement. All was not well though and the Archduke frowned upon hearing Ashley tell him that his parents were concerned about his budding talent, and about his growing friendship with the Archduke. They were worried that the Archduke would punish them for their son's skill, or would use it for his own gain, or, worst yet, that the Archduke had a plan to steal their son away and raise him as his own. There was a long moment of silence in the small conservatory where the two practiced their guitar playing and talked about music and its power and magic but that moment was broken and the Archduke finally spoke.

"Ashley, my name is Kelvin, and when we are together here, I want you to call me that. When you are here, I am no longer the Archduke, I am your friend. We have known one another long enough now that I want you to call me by my proper name. Will you do that for me? Will you call me Kelvin?"

Ashley looked at the Archduke a moment before putting his guitar down and held out his hand.

"Nice to meet you Kelvin, my name is Ashley, you can call me Ash."
The two smiled at one another and shook hands.

"We are well met then Ash. I want you to ask your parents to come to see me for dinner. They will be scared when you ask them this, and while I wish that wasn't so, for now, we'll let them be worried. I think that they, like so many others here, fear me. Do you know why that is?"

Ash thought a moment.

"Because you have power."

"Yes, they fear me because I have power, and I have abused my power for far too long. Once, I was like you - I was a boy full of hope and wonder, but I fell in love with the power I was offered and I lost my path, I lost my way, and now people fear me. They are right to be afraid of me, too. Once, I was a fearful man. Once, I was an angry man. Once, I was an awful man. But there came a day Ash, when I heard something that changed me, something beyond beauty, beyond words, something that woke up the sleeping boy in my heart and that thing was your voice. I was a bitter man for a great many years, and I have suffered for that. Now though, now I want to change, I need to. You see, what your parents and the others don't see is that they have power too. Everyone has power if they will but use it. But it is how you use that power that matters, not that you simply have it. I think that over the years I let myself fall in love with my power, and not the act of being powerful. Do you know what that means?"

Ash shook his head from side to side.

"What I mean is that I forgot to use my power responsibly. Instead of reaching out to people, to my people, I made rules and laws without thinking of their impact. I made it nearly impossible for people to reach me, to see me, and speak to me, and I made it so that people believed I was cold and cruel, when really, I was lonely. I forgot the words of my father, which he told me as I am telling this to you. He told me that power is nothing if you forget how to use it well. I had forgotten that simple lesson, forgotten it so long ago, but spending time with you here, and playing the music we have, I am remembering what I missed all these years and it has made me very, very sad."
A tear ran down Kelvin's face and Ash watched it wind its way down, wide-eyed.

"I, I am sorry arch…"

"No, Kelvin, call me Kelvin, and I don't *want* you to feel sorry. That's the problem. I have built myself a tower of rules and laws and have forgotten how to rule well. I have forgotten why I have the power, and what I need to do with it. And after I had done all that, had built these towers, I remembered what it was to be lonely, and I spent far too many years feeling sorry for myself. You've reminded me though what it was to be free, to be young, and to know who I am and what I am meant to do. Your gift has freed me of the arrogance I have been under the spell of for these many years. Your music Ash, your gift, it is that powerful, it is that special, but in being powerful, it is dangerous."

"Dangerous?"

"You can never forget why you have your gift Ash, nor how you should use it. The day you start taking your gift for granted will be a sorrowful day, and on that day you will find that your gift has left you. It's then that you'll truly be alone, as I was. This will be the bottom of a very deep hole for you, and you'll have a very long journey to dig yourself out of it. When you take your gift for granted, when you rely on it, when you take advantage of it, you lose your passion, and when you lose your passion you get lazy, and when that happens, you'll lose your gift completely. Do you understand?"

Ash looked at Kelvin a moment then nodded his head, and then shook his head from side to side. He thought he understood, he thought he knew what Kelvin was saying but just as he was starting to get it, it slipped away and fell like a pebble into a pond.

"I dunno. I think I understand, but then I also

don't get it. When I think I am getting it I lose it. I just don't know."

"Well, you will in time. You will. I only hope a day never comes where you take that gift for granted. Should it happen though, remember me, remember these times we have spent, and remember the lessons I am teaching you. For now though, I'd like to speak to your parents. They are the first test of many for me to pass. I have much to make amends for, and it's time for me to start digging out of my own hole."

"Test? What sort of test? Aren't you done with your schooling?"
Kelvin smiled and let out a laugh that was just as deep as his voice.

"Well, yes, I am. I am out of school, that's true, but this is a different sort of test that I have to take and it is safe to say that this is as important a test as I have ever taken. First though, I need to prove to your parents and to the rest of the people of these lands that I want to make sure they are happy, that they are well, and that I am here to help them. I need to let people know that my walls have fallen, that I have changed, and it's thanks to you and your music. Now that's real power Ash, the power to change a life. That's the greatest power of all. That is the power you have. Remember that."

Kelvin, the Archduke of the Dark Lands passed his first test wonderfully, letting himself laugh, talk, reminisce, and showing Ashley's parents that he wasn't at all as harsh as he'd been made out to be. Kelvin charmed Ashley's parents as he had charmed the boy – with an open, honest heart and an eager ear. When Ashley's father, Jacob, asked why there was the rule about shoes Kelvin laughed and told him that the fact was that it had been a joke he'd told one of his under-secretaries once when they had been writing some new laws up and the secretary had put that it among the others. "Obviously, they didn't get the joke." He said, laughing.

"It's time, I think, for a change. What do you say, Jacob, would you like to be the head of a new department? It'd be a big favor to me."

Jacob looked nervously to his wife.

"Uh, what sort of job is it that you're offering me?"

"Well," Kelvin replied. "How about head of the Complaints, Compliments, and Cannonballs Department?"

"We, uh, have cannonballs?" All three members of the Pickles family leaned closer.

Kelvin tried very hard to hide the laugh that was growing inside him but lost his fight.

"Uh, well, to be honest, I threw that in to even

things out a bit. It didn't quite sound right to have the Department of Complaints and Compliments. It needed more 'zazz', if you know what I mean. Though, maybe we can add some cannonballs around here just for looks. We can paint them, oh, I don't know, what do you think about the color purple?"

The four of them broke into great fits of laughter and the rest of the evening was spent talking about the plans for the Dark Lands, of music, of art, of the rumors that the Queen of the Kingdom of Man's daughter wasn't interested in being a Mistress of Magic herself, and finally, Kelvin and Ash sang and played guitar. It was an extraordinary evening and one Ashley and his family would never forget. While there was still a nagging question as to whether this was another trick from a man they had spent so many years distrusting, the Pickles family trusted their hearts and began trusting the Archduke.

That night, after the family had left, Kelvin began planning what changes he'd make to the Dark Lands, and there would be many. He was up the rest of that evening working on letters to the Queen and to other leaders in lands near and far on a strategy to make the people of the Dark Lands feel like they were a bigger part of things. After he had worked on all this he set about working on what he felt was perhaps most important thing of all, and that was on making sure that music and the arts would return to his lands and be taught once again to people of all ages. Once the Song Mothers had wandered the lands, spreading their gifts of music but those days had drawn to a close ages before and since then much music had left the lands, his being one of those that had lost it. He had been better at math than anything else but when he was taught guitar by a student of one of the Song Mother's when he was still a child new worlds had opened before him that he'd never imagined before. *Logic and Art*, he wrote, inspired and beginning work on a song for Ash, smiling into the darkness and the wonders of tomorrow. For Kelvin, the Archduke of the Dark Lands, it was a new beginning, and one that was long overdue.

The news came late to the Pickles family that the Archduke, that Kelvin, was dead. The political machinery of the Dark Lands had never made it easy to get the word out about things and, being that there had never been a village crier, and that the Archduke's staff was busy worrying over what to do next, not many knew about his passing for over a month. Those who had been in the Archduke's circle, those men and women who had hungered for his power, gathered and fought for days over who was to get what, to do what, and who would take over and during it all they hid the letters and ideas he had been working on, and filled the void he had left as quickly as possible. For them, this was perfect, and the longer it took the people to realize their leader was dead, the better. They would, they decided, rule as a group, and would take what the Archduke had done and would push forward with that world, making sure that their jobs were secure indefinitely. Before any word came down though, Ashley knew in his heart that his friend was gone. Kelvin had wanted a few days to work on some things so he gave Ash a guitar to practice with and told him to learn some new songs and that he would call for him when he was free again. The days passed and no word came and Ashley became worried. Days became a week, then a week and a half and clearly something was wrong, though his parents insisted otherwise. The boy felt that something was wrong when he would sit down to play guitar, which had been Kelvin's first guitar, and it was as if there was a block that wasn't letting him play anything. Everything he tried to play sounded off and he knew it in the places of the heart where all people know what is true and what is right and he finally had his reason why everything was off when his father returned from work one day saying that there was no such place as the Department of Complaints, Compliments, and Cannonballs. He had, it turned out, been laughed at when he suggested such a thing to someone in charge and that he was indeed in charge of the department. Defeated, Mr. Pickles had returned to his usual job, and started to worry, himself. Something really was wrong it would seem, and Ashley hadn't bee wrong to worry.

Over the next few days that vague worry the Pickles family had started to feel became a solid, dreadful thing as the news of the Archduke's death inched its way to the family. He was gone, they were finally told by their elderly neighbor - Kelvin was dead. The old miser had died and good riddance, the neighbor told the Pickles family, spitting as he said it on his way from a shared garden back to his small shack. The family was stunned by this grim news and the house fell into a deep silence that filled the air and weighed upon everyone's chests. Ashley took it hardest of all though and he looked to his mother and father and they opened their mouths to speak but there was nothing they could say, nothing they could do to take away the pain that was so vivid in their son's face. Ashley had been trying to play guitar near the door to the family home when the neighbor had paused long enough to tell them the news and suddenly the instrument felt as if it were a thousand pounds to him. And at that moment all Ash wanted was to drop it, to drop the guitar and never touch it again but try as he did, he *couldn't* drop it. He couldn't let it go. A hundred emotions filled him at once and all he wanted to do was run, to get away, so he turned from his parents and ran out of the yard and

through the tall weeds where some Ghost Worms were trying starting to emerge, guitar still held firm in his hand. His mother and father moved to the door and could only watch as their son ran from them and into the night, knowing he needed time, needed space, and needed the dark.
And so Ashley embraced the darkness, and as a fine mist fell, it embraced him back.

And away, far away, Ashley ran, the cool air good on his burning skin but it didn't calm the fire that raged in his heart and veins. He ran and ran until his legs would carry him no further and he finally fell beside a small lake, beneath a great tree, and then everything turned to tears as he fell into the grass.

Ashley awoke several hours later and the air was cold the moon was high, and there was fog everywhere making it hard to see. Ash sat up and wiped dew from his face and looked out over the lake and toward the sound of something moving. One of the pond's creatures raised its head from the water and it let out a mournful call before diving back into the depths and that sound filled Ash's head and heart and perfectly expressed what he felt now. He sat a moment, as that sound rattled around his head and then, almost absently, picked up his guitar and started playing. He first played something near to the sound he heard, and then started adding to it, bit by bit, and as he added to it, words formed on his tongue that begged to be uttered, words that linked and connected and wound around the music and which became a song about the Archduke and about losing one's chance to make amends for the wrongs they have done in life. It was well into dawn when he finished his song and when he had finished he looked up to see almost a dozen Bumble Kitties purring in the tree above him, their eyes on him and their attention on the song. Ash would have kept playing but as he played he couldn't shake the feeling that the purring of the kitties was connecting to his song and as he was trying to figure out if that was by chance or design he realized he'd stopped playing. As soon as he stopped, the kitties began crying for more and he had to laugh as he got up and made his way back home and they tried to give chase after him. Ashley laughed again when he saw that all of them, upon giving up, returned to the tree beside the lake, perhaps deciding this was a fine new home or maybe just too lazy to return to where they'd come from.

Ashley sang the song he'd just written to himself as he made his way home and as he wandered through the village toward his home several people heard it and started following the boy with the beautiful voice and the sorrowful song. Most didn't know who the boy was but his song was such that they were compelled to follow, unable to stop their feet from moving. The people

followed Ashley the many miles until he was home again, none of them saying a word, lest they break the spell, and when the boy's mother and father answered the knock at their door they let out a joyful sob on seeing their son but were shocked to see the many people that had come with him. To Mister and Missus Pickles it looked as if half the whole village had followed their son home. Ash, not having realized this, turned and saw them all and was amazed to see the mass of people but had to wonder who they were and why were they here?
There was an awkward silence as the Ash and his parents looked at the people and the people looked back at them but a woman from the village finally approached the young man –

"Please forgive us this trespass my friends. We were all doing our daily chores when each of us heard your son's song and, hearing it, all troubles seemed to melt away. We all wanted to hear more of it so we followed him here. It's such a beautiful, sad song; won't you please sing it again my boy? Please?"

Ash was stunned. He hadn't even realized he'd *been* singing all these miles and he blushed and looked to his parents not quite sure what to do. His parents, not even knowing their son had *written* a song let alone that all these strangers had heard it, asked the same question the rest of the villagers had –

"Will you play us the song?"

Ash, suddenly embarrassed and shy, looked around and saw so many people, more people than he'd ever played for before, more people than he'd ever even *dreamed* of playing for and he didn't know if he could do it. He didn't know if he could sing with this much pressure on him, or this many eyes. He was lost for a moment, uncertain what to do, uncertain what to say but suddenly, he knew. He would do what Kelvin would have wanted him to do - he would share his gift. This was the Archduke's song, this was for him, so for him would Ash sing, and these people could watch if they wished.

Ashley walked away from the house and to a large oak tree and where there was a large, flat red stone, and he sat upon this stone and he began to play. As Ash played he felt such clean, free, and it was as if no one watching him at all and it was just he and Kelvin's guitar, just he and *his* guitar. He sang as he'd never sung before, played as he'd never played and, when he was done, he found he was crying. It was the greatest feeling in the world, because for those moments it was about the music, the song, and about his lost friend. Then it was gone as he remembered where he was, and that he was playing for so many people and he rubbed away his tears, hoping no one had seen but, when he looked out at the people, he realized they none had seen anything because they were crying too. He stood up and walked slowly to his house, exhausted and needing to rest, but as he made it to the door, someone spoke up and he turned to them to see who it was. It was a young girl, no more than four, and she was standing toward the back of the crowd, one hand wiping tears away while her mother held her other. The girl came forward until finally she was standing before Ashley and she spoke again.

"Who…I mean, if I may ask, who was that song about? Did you write it about someone? Or *for* someone?"

Everyone's eyes were on him, awaiting his answer and suddenly all of the worry was gone as he smiled at her –

"I wrote that for Archduke Kelvin, a very good man, and someone I loved. He is no longer with us, and I wrote it for him. He was a good man."

With that, he turned away from everyone, walked into his home, and as soon as he was in his small room, he lay down his guitar, fell upon his bed, and slept for three days straight.

Ashley woke those three days after his

performance to a new world, a new life, and a legend that he could never have dreamed. While he'd slept, people from across the Kingdom of Man had come and surrounded the simple home of his family and all of them were awaiting news about the boy with the remarkable voice. Ashley was shocked by all of the people in his yard and around his house and couldn't believe they were all there for him. Ash's parents, uncertain what to do, felt that he must decide for himself what he wanted to do about the people. If he wanted to be left alone then his mother and father would go out and ask the people to leave, but if he wanted to sing then here was his audience, waiting with eager ears. Ash looked out a window at the crowd and smiled. There were even more people here than there had been before and that meant more people to tell the tale of the Archduke. Kelvin had never gotten a chance to tell his story, or to make amends for all he had done and this was Ash's chance to let people know about the real man, and not just the man people believed him to be.

His smile widened.

He picked up his guitar, kissed his mother and father on their cheeks, and walked out into the courtyard to greet his audience.

The days and weeks passed like this, with Ash leaving every morning to sing for the people and coming inside only when the sun had fallen, the air had chilled, and he could no longer stay awake. Each day the crowds grew and with each performance word spread further and further until all people in the realm had heard of the boy with the voice that could charm the very stars in the sky. At first Ashley had intended to play only the one song, the ode to the Archduke Kelvin but it wasn't long until the people began to want more, demanded more, so reluctantly he would sing other songs he knew, other favorites, and a ten minute performance quickly became a half an hour, then an hour, and eventually the entire day, with Ash only taking occasional breaks for food and rest. It was amazing to Ash, all of it, and the applause from the people shook the hills and rumbled the ground as Ashley stumbled back to his home. Weary as he was, Ashley was always bolstered by the cheering and by the hope that his words would change how people viewed Kelvin and might make them question what they'd been told about him.

And so the days passed, Ashley singing to the people five of the seven days, and taking Saturday and Sunday to rest. He had told his parents that he was just going out to sing that first day, to give the people what they wanted but day gave to day gave to day and each day he told Mr. and Mrs. Pickles the same thing – he couldn't let Kelvin down. The days passed to weeks, to months, to years and letting Kelvin down became letting 'the people' down, which one day turned to him telling them that he was born to sing. Time passed and suddenly Ashley was thirteen and the people were more enchanted by his voice than ever.

All this time Ashley had held true to what Kelvin had taught him, all this time he never took a gift, never forgot that his voice *was* his gift, and always made sure to tell the people about Kelvin, the man that had inspired his most beloved song. It was when he was thirteen though when he first took something for his singing. Something he didn't need, but wanted just the same. Oddly, this too was the first day he'd forgotten to tell the people who Kelvin was, and that his song was about anyone in particular at all.

Ashley took his schooling at home, his mother having had to leave her job in order to make sure that there was someone to help out with the steadily growing crowds that surrounded the family home. Bureen Pickles, Ash's mother, made sure though, no matter how much time Ash spent on performing, that she taught him lessons about the history, the world, the universe, and that he learned something new every day. Things were hard for the family but what the family lost in income they gained in donations of food from the people who had made the long trip to see Ashley. At times it was almost as if people had come to see the whole family, the way the visitors reacted. Bread, fish, meat, drink, ale, and exotic foods the family had never even heard of appeared at their back door every morning and each night the family would take the invitation of a passerby and they would all dine together and hear wonderful tales of the world beyond the Dark Lands. These dinners, as much as the Pickles family loved them, ended after the first year when it became clear that the people were not as interested in the companionship and storytelling as much as they wanted a private audience with Ashley and wanted the prestige of such a thing. Things finally got out of hand when people tried to sneak into the house then. Ashley's father was forced to build a great fence to surround the house, and things really seemed to change for the family after that fence went up. Too many people had started living on the land of the Pickles and this had lead to several fights between the visitors over who would set their camp closest to the house so Mr. Pickles knew something else must be done.

The fence wasn't enough.

Mr. Pickles, with the help of some friends from his work, built a small area away from the house where people would be able to sit for Ashley's performances. It was a simple thing, but it made a difference, and took away much of the family's stress. At the same time though, it also seemed to change things.

It certainly changed Ashley.

The stage consisted of the flat rock (now

polished to a shine) where Ash would sit beneath his favorite tree, an area where he could have some space from the crowds and then there were benches for the crowds, or some of them at least. The formality of a stage though put a swagger in Ash's step, and made him savor the applause perhaps a moment longer than he did before, bowing now as he stood on the rock before *and* after his performance.

Ash was changing, day by day, and no one was noticing.

Despite the changes in Ash, the family had managed to remain modest despite their growing fame or rather the growing fame of their son, but that modesty was slipping. The family was getting so much food that they didn't quite know what to do with it and, instead of letting it go to waste, began distributing it to the local people who were not as fortunate, from the back of their home. They felt good about giving much of the food away, like that was the right thing to do, and it was. It was a good time, but as more time passed, Ashley's singing began to take over more and more of his family's lives, and thus saw less and less of the world outside of his performances. His father could barely pass a day without someone wanting to talk to him about his son, or someone trying to curry special favors from the family, saw a private show or better seats. Mr. Pickles' superiors tried this as well, telling him that it might be in his family's best interest to arrange a private performance for the new Council of Laws and Things, which had taken over for the Archduke. Mr. Pickles politely put the question aside each time but there came a time when he finally told them know and he was told that he was no longer needed. Mr. Pickles was stunned.

He couldn't believe they'd go that far, firing him because he wouldn't allow his son to sing for them, and them alone. And suddenly here he was, out of work and unsure what came next. He questioned his decision as he walked home that evening, reasoning that they *were* the new people in charge of things that maybe…but he couldn't have done it, he couldn't take advantage of his son's gift that way. And that was when he lied to his son for the first time. He didn't have the heart to tell Ash the truth of what had happened so he and his wife told the boy that he was on an extended leave which, Ash never noticed, never came to an end.

Time passed.

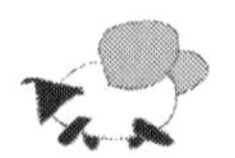

It was just after Ash's thirteenth birthday that things really started to change for Ash, and when he took his first steps away from the path Kelvin had set him on. Ash had just finished another performance and was feeling rather like he was the king of all that he surveyed when a young woman came forward and dropped a package onto the stage near his feet then turned and was lost in the crowds. At this point, people had taken up camping on the land that surrounded Ash's family and those that couldn't fit were renting space on the farmland of the neighbors, and the crowds had gotten so thick that Ash wasn't able to get five feet before he was besieged by people who wanted to speak to him, to touch him, to have him sing *their* songs. Ash moved back to his stage and the people stopped following, held back by the simple wood barrier and the thin line that separated people from beasts. Ash reached down and picked up the gift, not sure what else to do, and examined it. The audience assumed he was on another break so they started to go off for food or began to talk amongst themselves, giving Ash a moment to see what he'd been given. The gift was wrapped in thin blue tissue paper and smelled of perfume that pulled a smile to his mouth. Ash carefully unwrapped the gift and found inside it a beautiful red scarf that looked to be made of exotic silks and which had a golden ***A*** stitched onto it. Ash let out a gasp and pulled the scarf to his chest, looking around to make sure no one had seen him. When he was satisfied, he held it up to his face and it was softer than anything he'd ever felt before. He looked around again and saw no one looking and, before he knew what he was doing, he had pushed the scarf deep into his pocket and smiled to himself.

Ash didn't know why he had taken it but he had. He took it because it was beautiful, because it was soft, and because he wanted it. It had just been his birthday after all, so this was just a present.
Wasn't it?
Wasn't it?

Thirteen became fourteen, turned fifteen, and when Ashley's sixteenth birthday came the crowds were as large as ever. Land and a stage made of fine, imported woods had been donated by a neighbor on their property (thus encouraging people to pay to tent there to 'be closer to the voice of the angels') so Ash played there and now thousands of people could see him. Another neighbor had offered to lend Ash a magical voice amplifier so he wouldn't have to strain his voice when he sang and so now his songs reached the people, all of the people, with ease. In exchange for this wondrous device, all the man asked was for a good word from Ash during his shows about how delicious the neighbor's dairy and meat were, which were both for sale at a nearby stand. Tents were provided for people so they could get out of the rain, for a fee, of course, and that was another person he had thank during his performance. Then there were the outfits that a local seamstress had made for Ashley, insisting that he must be *seen* if he was to perform before so many people. How would the people see him and know it was he, and not an imposter? This sounded reasonable to Ash, though he'd never heard of anyone pretending to be him but, you never quite knew so he agreed to accept her clothes in exchange for a few words about how durable and inexpensive they were. His guitar too had been replaced with one fitted with jewels which the maker told Ash were to help sweeten the sound, and again, this was given free, if he would but tell the people what true sound it gave off. The guitar was the hardest thing to convince Ashley to take but, after many weeks, he agreed to use it and put his own guitar in its case for the first time in six years. These were but a few of the many people who had found ways to get a piece of Ashley's gift and bit by bit his talent and his promises to Kelvin began to dim. Ashley paid no mind to all of that though, as he was too focused on putting together new song lists to sing for the people so they wouldn't get bored and lose interest in him, always making sure to end with their favorite, the song of the man who had lost his last chance. The song had once been called *For the Archduke Kelvin, Upon His Dying*, but was now known as *Ashley's Song*, as that's how people referred to it. And it mattered little to Ash what it was called, so long as the people knew it, sang it, and loved it.

Ah, but what of his parents?

Ash's parents were not happy when he began taking the gifts from the neighbors and villagers but he was able to justify it by simply telling them that he was sharing their wealth. He was helping others with his talent, and wasn't that what he *should* do? They didn't have the heart to argue with that and, it *was* his gift, after all, and he could do what he wanted with it. They too had been guilty of accepting food, drink, clothes, and shoes when they'd been offered, feeling that they had sacrificed so much to make sure their son succeeded that it was only fair. And as soon as they had accepted these gifts it was easier to accept it when he began taking his gifts, and then began to take gifts of money or other goods from the strangers who came to hear him sing. They were just showing their appreciation for his gift, was what he'd tell them, and they agreed, though begrudgingly. As time passed though, Ashley began to see less and less of his parents as others from the village, mainly members of the Council of Laws, began keeping the crowds back, accepting the gifts, and making his plans for him and in the end, there was little need for Ash's parents to be involved with things anymore. There was little for them to do and members of the Council insisted that it was time for them to rest and take ease in their lives, though they were only in the forties so they supported their son the best way they were able – with love. For their love, Mr. and Mrs. Pickles were allowed to remain on their land, were given food every week, and were allowed five hours a week with their son, unless, that is, he was busy. Things remained this way until Ashley Pickles was seventeen, when things finally changed.

As much as Ash loved performing, doing it seven days a week had become too much for him and he felt as if he was missing something of life. It didn't feel like this was *his* life anymore but rather the life of those around him. He was performing for them, not himself anymore. He had heard from members of the audience that there were fees being charged to see Ashley now, though he had never been told of such a thing, and certainly never made any money from the performances. To back that up, each day it seemed a new dignitary or someone of wealth, bravery, or fame was sitting there in the first few rows, which had plush seats and which were raised up so they had a better view than the rest of the audience. When Ash had asked about this he was told that these were matters for a group called the Council for Ashley Pickles and His Beloved Voice to deal with, and that he needn't worry about it. Still though, it bothered him. To ease his mind of all its worries the Council for Ashley Pickles gave Ash a small cottage near the stage where he could stay so he wouldn't have to make the 'exhausting travel' to his parents' home every night. This seemed silly to Ash and he thanked the members of his Council when he told them this, just as he told them that he had a place to live, with his parents, and that he was happy there. Not a day after he'd said that though

he found he was requested for dinners with people who had come to see him from afar about his gift and about the magic he was giving the world. He felt obligated to accept these dinners and, when they began to last longer and longer, dipping deep into the night, it just seemed the most convenient thing in the world to stay in the cottage he'd been given, planning to stay there just for the night. Within a month staying in the cottage had become a habit and this had become his new home and it was a rare occasion indeed that he even saw his parents or anyone from his past.
There was just no time for that, anymore.

Still though, as much as he loved the luxury, the attention, and the fame, he longed for a day to himself. Just one day off. Begrudgingly the Council gave it to him, telling Ash he could take Sunday for himself, to do as he would, but *only* Sunday, and that he'd have to play an extra show on Saturday to make up for it.

That one free day out of the week was a gift like none Ash had ever received before. He would play the week's shows as they were scheduled – one in the morning and one in the evening with lunches and meetings with dignitaries between – and then on Sunday he'd sneak out of the small village to be alone for a few hours. He snuck out hidden beneath a thick gray cloak, and returned to the lake that had first inspired him so long ago. The lake was as he had remembered it despite the many years he'd been absent. What amused him most was that the tree he had once sat beneath was full to overflowing with Bumble Kitties of every shape and size. If only the silly, lazy things had spread themselves out they could all have lived among the many trees that stood around the lake but Bumble Kitties were known not for their ambition but for their great laziness and their relaxing purr so it was no surprise to find so many nestled in the great tree. As it was the great tree bent from the weight of the kitties, who upon seeing Ash, took flight and surrounded him with their furry faces and buzzing purrs. Ash had to admit that he hadn't been looking to spend his day off with anyone, man or beast, but the kitties were soothing and seemed to take all his troubles and worries away, which wasn't a bad thing at all.

Each Sunday Ashley would return to that lake and his new Bumble Kitty friends, his old guitar in tow, with the hopes of creating more music to play for the people, and perhaps getting some much needed rest. He had played all of the songs he knew so many times that he could sense that he was starting to lose the audience, and that it was time for some new material. He had meant to write new songs since Kelvin had died and he'd just never found the time, ambition, or the reason. He was getting worried though and now was as good a time as any to start writing new music. The trouble was though that whenever he'd sit down beneath the tree and start playing something the kitties would start their purring and in no time he'd be lost in that sound and would put his guitar down and fall asleep for the remainder of the day. Each time this happened Ashley would become furious at the Bumble Kitties, who, once he'd stopped playing, lost interest in him and would return to their tree. He'd yell at the kitties, would shake their tree, and would swear he wouldn't return to that lake, that tree, and to the awful influence of those kitties but each Sunday he'd return, bright and early and acting as if nothing had happened the week before to upset him. As much as he tried to deny the fact, Ash loved the undivided attention of the kitties and, as he lost the attention of his audience, the kitties were still for him and always wanting more. The kitties craved his music no matter what he played so they soon became his greatest fans.

Returning to the stage after those peaceful Sundays became harder and harder for Ashley because each performance he felt as if he was losing more and more of his audience, and, from what he heard from the Council, this was indeed true. It seemed that there was a young boy who had taken to singing near a well in a neighboring village and it was said that he had a voice that rivaled Ash's. Ash laughed when he heard this, as did his attendants, but there was no mistaking the restlessness that took to his audiences when he stretched his performances to three hours and took much of that added hour to sell goods and services and to talk about how special and rare his voice and talent was. This last bit wasn't something from the script he was given before each performance but was something he added himself and which frustrated the Council as they felt that a large part of his appeal was how humble he was and his speeches were becoming far from humble. He told the Council that he appreciated their opinion and would think on what they said but that his voice was a gift, and people needed to remember that and appreciate it. This happened on a Sunday and, though he certainly intended to think about what they were telling him, by the time he got to the lake and had started to pluck at his guitar he was growing tired again and fell asleep to the sound of the purring kitties without giving his ego a second thought.

The Council was growing tired of the boy.

The Great Council, as it had come to be known, had made a great deal of money from Ashley and his singing and they had filled their pockets with the riches and they were none too anxious to lose out on that but his attitude and performances were steadily declining. Greater than the riches was having the attention of the dignitaries and famed people who had come to the Dark Lands to hear Ashley sing. With these new friendships much had been done to guarantee that The Great Council would not lose its standing and power any time soon. With no heir to the Archduke and the help of the other areas to make sure no one called for a new head of power, their place was secured, or so it seemed. The Council feared that if their young singer started to lose favor with the audience, and, in turn, with the visiting guests that they would lose any backing they might need should an heir to the Archduke be found or should someone ask for a new head of the Dark Lands. Needing a solution to their problem, the Council sent for the young boy they had heard about who sang near the well. They had to hear for themselves whether his voice was as magical as some said it was.

And much as people had felt when they first heard young Ashley so many years earlier, when they heard the boy for the first time the members of the Council were astounded that such beauty could come from such a young person and it was their tears that told the tale, and which sealed Ash's fate. The decision was made before the boy had finished his song – a change would be made.

Ashley was told the next day that, after so many years of loyal service, he was being given Saturday off as well. Ash was a bit shocked at this but felt that yes, he *had* been working very hard, and it *was* time that he took some time for himself. He'd see his family more, he'd spend more time with friends he'd lost track of and, more than anything, it'd give him time to work on new material. It bothered him to no end that he had been relying on the works of others for so long and since the day he'd written his song for the Archduke he'd wanted to write more music but had never found the time. Now was his chance. Ash rarely saw his parents anymore, really had no more friends after so many years of not speaking to them, and the music, the music seemed more distant than ever to him. It was time to get back to his roots. When Ashley told himself all of this he had meant it, every word of it, but, well, things didn't quite work out the way we plan sometimes.

He was on the way to his parent's home the first Saturday he had off when he happened to wonder whether he'd left his lucky red scarf near the waters of the lake the previous Sunday and naturally, he had to go and look and see. It was only when he sat down to take a few minutes to rest that he realized that he was still wearing the scarf, which made him laugh. He was tired after the long walk so he decided to sit for a moment and he started plucking at his guitar absently, thinking about a home cooked dinner, about his father's harmonica playing, and thinking about how comfortable the rocking chair on the back porch would be, but before he knew it, he was fast asleep and dreaming about visiting his parents and spending the evening with them instead of doing it. When he awoke it was past nine at night and he'd slept the entire day away. He frowned and looked down at his guitar, which felt heavier than usual. Sitting in the hole in the belly of the guitar was a Bumble-Kitty, asleep and purring, its wings folded neatly on its back. Ashley looked down on it and any anger he had melted away. He laid the guitar gently on the grass and picked up the small kitty and placed it into a thick tumble of dandewillows. It was October; a week before the Harvest Festival, and the ground was getting thick with the leaves. He should sing some fun harvest songs, and maybe some about the Haunt Festival that came weeks afterward. Ash frowned then, remembering the festival and that this year it fell on a Saturday and wondered what the Council would do. He laughed. Well, they'd just move the festival to Friday, naturally. They couldn't have a festival without him now, could they? Why, it wasn't a festival without *Reaping Song*, or without *My Love Lay Under the Reap*, two songs he performed beautifully, if he did say so himself. Sure, he wouldn't have any *new* reap songs, as he'd promised the Council and the audience the year before but, if he felt up to it, maybe he'd pull out the old mandolin he'd been given by that nice couple from, hm, oh from somewhere, and he'd play a few songs on that. He wasn't as comfortable on a mandolin as he was his guitar but, well, he'd master it without much problem, he was sure of that.

Ash was laughing, singing an upbeat version of his song for the Archduke as he headed back to his home in the chilly night. He'd go see his parents the next day and tell them he'd been writing music all day and had lost track of time. Sure, that was exactly what he'd do. It was these thoughts that wandered through his head as he made his way back home but as he was walking he noticed that there was some sort of light coming from the performance area. He stopped a moment and squinted off into the distance, hoping to see what was happening. It looked, at least from here, that there were people on the stage, that there was an audience, and that, if he listened closely, it sounded like there was music coming from the area.
What?
How could this be?

Ashley found himself running, even as he tried to slow down, as if his feet and legs had minds of their own and were dragging him forward. A sick feeling flooded Ash's belly as he neared the noise and the stage. The magic lamps made it hard to see the audience but he could see the stage without a problem – there was a boy, a young boy, on it and playing a squeezebox and singing. And my, what a voice he had, a voice like Ash had never heard before. Around him were several people in the finery

of visiting guests, and they were singing too. Ash stopped running at the edge of the stage, behind a small tent used to sell commemorative stones with his face on them, stopped dead when he heard this stranger, this *boy* singing the song about the Archduke. This was not a mournful or sad song though but one which celebrated the life of a man this boy could have never known. The way this boy sang it, the song was not about a lost chance, but about the realization that you *have* more than one chance, and that you can change the world with that chance. He had made what had been a lament a song of redemption and joy. Ash even found himself tearing up and wasn't sure if it was the song or the sight before him.
The song ended and the night was filled with the roar of the crowd. He looked out from behind the tent, towards the audience and it was filled to well beyond capacity, which were far more people than Ash had seen here in some time. Someone on the stage called for the crowd to hush and Ash turned his attention back that way as well.

"Please, please, could we have some silence? Thank you, one and all, for coming out, yet again, to hear this wonderful, talented boy sing his song. It's only been three weeks and we've already had to expand to Saturdays *and* Sundays. The way it looks, he'll be playing seven days a week in no time. Would you like that?"

The crowd exploded with applause and whistling.

"We thought as much. Well, let's ask young master Glen, would *you* like to play here more often?"

The boy looked down at his feet and scuffed the toes of his shoes against the wood. After a moment he looked up at the head of The Great Council and answered.

"I would most surely love to sing here every day but I don't wanna get in the way of master Ashley and his playing. He's got the voice of an angel. In fact, it's him that inspired me to…"

"Good, good, good, so that's a yes. Isn't that great news, everyone?"
The crowd cheered again.

"OK, we'll start getting young master Glen out here singing every day of the week in no time at all. First though, let's talk about our annual reaping celebration - the Harvest Festival - that will be happening this next Saturday. We have some special things in store for all of you, which naturally means we will have to charge just a *little* extra but it will be worth it because that night centers around young master Glen and his magical songs…"

Ashley didn't hear anything else after that. He'd

fallen to his knees and was cradling his guitar, feeling like someone had punched him in the stomach. He didn't feel sad; he didn't feel upset, in fact, he felt nothing but the emptiness of shock. Nearby though there were more voices, and these voices from the crowd shook him from his stupor.

"Powerful voice that lad has. Real powerful voice." Said an older man.

"Reminds me of a young Ashley Pickles, he does." Said a woman.

"Nay, this boy has the voice of an angel, but that Pickles, well, he has the voice of an old, wooden trombone." Said another voice that could have been either a man *or* a woman.

"That doesn't make a lick of sense, Tops, not a lick of sense at all. The boy has talent, there's no doubt, and a voice a sweet as can be, but what he lacks is that song, that one, sweet song that made Ashley so special when I first saw him so many years ago." Ash smiled weakly when he heard this.

"Aye, that was a song alright, but the boy, that Glen, can sing it too. And sing it sweeter. What was that old song about, anyway? I never could figure it out. Someone said it was about the Queen over there where the sun shines, the one with the weird daughter." Said the first man again.

"Naw, it was about *him*, that's who. It was about Ashley. He saw the day when he wasn't gonna be the one in the spotlight and it was about…"

"You're both all wet," said a woman. "It was about that good for nothing Archduke we had for so long. It was a song about that old man and the opportunity he missed. It was about a crummy man that screwed up everyone's lives."

"Ohhhhhh." Said all the voices in unison.

"Shhh, shush down now, they're gonna get back to the music." This was a girl that couldn't have been much older than the boy on stage and with that, the voices quieted and the cheering began again.

Ashley tried to stand, couldn't, and fell to his knees again. He knelt there, the world swirling, and watched, the sound around him becoming deafening. He felt like he was being buried in music, as if he was being suffocated by it. He closed his eyes and stood again, slowly this time, and he finally made it to his feet. He picked up his guitar as he moved to a standing position and stood there a moment, trying to get his balance. The music got louder, he opened his eyes and the lights felt like they were burning into him. He felt ill. He had to move, he had to leave, he

had to get away.
And he had to go now.
He closed his eyes against the stage and the crowd and moved forward, towards where his mother and father lived. Towards a safe place. He heard people call out to him and when he did he moved with more speed and eventually he opened his eyes and found he was at the door of his childhood home. He let out a sob and started knocking. He heard nothing and no one came to the door. He knocked again and again there was but silence. He took a step away from the door and looked at it, wondering if he'd somehow found the wrong house but, as he stared at the door he realized there was a note taped to it -

Ashley, you didn't show up for lunch today so we've gone to see the new Queen's coronation. They say she's ***magic,*** *and has a gift like you do -. I wonder if you two should speak some day. Love you, mom and dad.*

Ash didn't return to his cottage that night but returned instead to the lake, to the tree, and to the Bumble Kitties whose purring let him forget his pain and the feeling of confusion that had suddenly filled him. And as he lay there, under the stars, wrapped in a blanket of leaves, the sounds of the kitties followed him into a world of nightmare sleep.

Ashley spent the following days at the lake, washing there, taking fruit from the surrounding trees to eat, and sleeping beneath the trees that had become the home of at least three tribes of Bumble Kitties. Some days he would lie on his back and look up into the sky, a sky where the stars were always somewhat visible, and would wonder what it would be like to live somewhere else. Somewhere sunny. Somewhere different. He had finally seen the Meep Sheep he'd heard of in the village as they made their way across the sky, going from here to there and from there to here. As much as he wished for them though, not one came to him, and this was a source of even more sadness for him. But, he thought, deep down in the place where he knew more than he'd like to believe, it meant something. It meant something that they didn't come to him, and if he could figure out *what* it meant, then maybe he'd have an answer to why he felt so alone and distant.

After he had been gone for several days he became surprised that no one had come looking for him and decided that, in the end, he may have done everyone a favor by disappearing. It was better he disappear on his own than force them to ask him to relinquish the stage and give up his audience.

His audience.

He cringed every time those words played through

his head. He had learned, if nothing else, in the time since he'd found about the other singer, something of how self indulgent and arrogant he'd become. He had taken the scarlet scarf off the first night he was there, having caught his reflection in the water and realizing how silly he looked in it. He was realizing a lot about how he'd spent the past years while he was away from everything. What had hit him hardest of all was how he had failed the Archduke, his friend, in so many ways. He had been so proud of his song, of how it gave honor to the man that had meant so much to him but now wondered if he had just used the death of his friend as a way to write a song. He started to wonder if he'd used the death of Kelvin to make the people love him all the more, remembering how he'd tear up after he played the song and knowing that, after the first few times, the tears were for show and effect and not from real sadness. Worse even than that though, he had failed to wield his gift responsibly. He'd written one song and had sat upon it and remained there until he was pushed from it by someone else. He had never tried, at least not very hard, to make new music. He had lived off of the talent and music of others. He had even stopped trying to connect with the people.
In the end, he'd forgotten what it was like to want for something, to struggle for something and had even forgotten how hard his parents had worked to make sure the family had what it needed before and after his fame. He'd forgotten his parents and when

they had stopped appearing at his shows, when they had stopped trying to see him at his cottage he had chalked it up to their jealousy of his fame.
He had chalked up a lot of things to that.
Such as how no one he had grown up with had kept in touch with him over the years. And how people had taken to whispering about him as he passed. Jealous, he'd thought, they were all jealous of him, but were they?
Or was it just that he wasn't the same person as the boy that once loved to sing and make people happy?

These thoughts and a hundred others plagued Ash as he wasted away the days by the water. He had stopped playing his guitar because it felt too heavy and full of too many lies and had stopped singing because his mouth was always dry. He had gone by his cottage a few times to get clothes but had gone late in the evening, when no one was around to see him. He had tried to return once, the day he'd let his mind wander over all he'd been through and had heard a great many voices coming from the place and, as he neared, he realized why – the Great Council had taken it upon themselves to continue using his cottage as a meeting and eating place and it was now young Glen that was the center of attention, and it would seem it was he and his father that were now living there. That was the last time he'd returned to his cottage and he couldn't say he was sad about that.

Ash did a great many things during this time but all of these were things that lead him away from the paths that might give him answers. In fact, he did everything possible to *avoid* thinking about the question he must answer before all others – *what now?* But one can put such a question off only so long until finally, there is no choice but to address it. It was time to address it.

It had been two weeks and Ashley had reached the end of his lying to himself. He couldn't stand the isolation and loneliness anymore. He couldn't stand the shame he felt. He looked at the guitar and he knew what he had to do, where he had to start and just as he was about to act, on instinct more than anything else, one of the Bumble Kitties plopped itself down atop the guitar and meowed at him for attention. Suddenly all of the anger and frustration he'd been feeling boiled over and he leaned forward and grabbed the Bumble Kitty up and stood in one fluid motion. Without even thinking he threw the animal out over the lake and turned away and waited to hear the splash of its landing.

*It was their fault. Those awful animals. It was their fault he couldn't write songs. It was their fault he'd not been at the stage singing but here, sleeping. It was their...*but before he could finish that thought he realized that there had *been* no splash. There had been no sound at all. His heart dropped and he opened his eyes and moved for the lake to save the Bumble Kitty in case it couldn't swim, but to his shock the fluffy creature was hovering mere inches from the water and pawing at its reflection in the lake as if it were another kitty, a water kitty. Its orange wings, so much like those of a butterfly, beat slow but strong, keeping the bumble-kitty aloft as it stared at its distorted image in the water. In a moment it grew bored of this game and flew forward and spun around in a lazy circle, flew upside-down for a moment, then made its way back to shore and dropped back to the grass and looked up to Ash and meowed, as if nothing at all had happened.

"You were able to fly like that this whole time?"

He looked up into the tree for an answer, and a hundred other Bumble Kitties looked down at him with sleepy eyes.

"You, you silly things can really fly? Not just a few feet but can really fly. But if that's they case why don't you, why don't you just…"
Then it was clear to him. Everything was clear to him.

Everything.

Laziness. They didn't fly because they were lazy, and that was it. They could fly all over the Kingdom, he guessed, if they had a need or desire to, but they were usually just happy buzzing around the same areas because it was easier to do.
And then there was Ashley, who had had all the time he wanted to write new songs but had chosen instead to sleep, to daydream, to play with the Bumble Kitties, and to spend too much time being adored by his fans that he'd never made the time to write his songs. He'd had dozens of ideas; he just never thought any of them would be what the 'people' wanted to hear so he let the ideas wither on the vine and lived off of the music of other people. It was him, not the kitties, not the Great Council, not the audience, and not some boy - it was him, Ashley Pickles that was responsible for where he was today. He had done this to himself. He'd taken the applause, he'd taken the gifts, and he'd taken all of it except the criticism. And there had been criticism. He had heard people say that he relied too much on other people's songs. He had heard it said that he was insincere. He had even heard his own parents tell him that it was about time he thought about what came next, told to him on his seventeenth birthday, the last day he'd really spent any time with them, which he now remembered bitterly, wondering if that was why he had not gone to see them in so long.

Ash felt overwhelmed again and wanted to run; run as far away as he could, as fast as he was able but instead of running he stood still and stared at the guitar. He had run before, and he saw where it had gotten him – lonely, hungry, and lost in his own homeland. No, this was the time to stand and face his action.

Now was the time to do something.

Really do something.

Ashley bent down and picked up his guitar and found it really wasn't so heavy after all, in fact, it felt lighter than it ever had. He stood a moment, waiting for inspiration to strike him and all of a sudden it did, in the form of something familiar, but so mysterious. He had to laugh as he began playing a song, a new song, and making up lyrics as he went along. Before he knew it, the Bumble Kitties were singing along to his song in their own way and it was their buzzing purr that pushed him on and inspired him further and just like that, the Bumble Kitties inspired Ash to start over and get back to where he was meant to be. Their purring joining his song, matching it, pushing it, echoing it and the trees around the lake shaking with the music of the many kitties as they sang with him.

And so the hours passed.

It was almost a full day before Ashley stopped playing his guitar and singing, time flying by and blurring and he anxious to keep playing. He had never worked harder, or for as long, and when he finally stopped long enough to take a break he had never been happier. He wasn't sure how many songs he'd written but they were there, in his hands, in his mouth, in his heart. They were part of him now and waiting to be set free. The rumbling purr of the Bumble Kitties had served as a sort of backing rhythm that pushed the music forward and kept Ashley working. Their buzzing had inspired him instead of putting him to sleep. It was almost as if they were the sounds of an inner engine that pushed him onward. He opened his hands and laid the guitar down, wincing at the pain but smiling through it. It seemed he wasn't the only one ready for a rest as around him lay the slumbering kitties, their wings fluttering from time to time in their sleep. He reached out and ran his hand over a napping Bumble Kitty and its wings opened and fluttered in appreciation. Ash looked out over the lake and saw it was late in the day, near to dusk, and the butterbugs and willow-wills were lighting up the shores and casting their orange and blue lights across the grass and the water. He still had a lot of work ahead of him, this was just the beginning and he knew it, but

for now, it was time to stop working on the songs, and time to work on himself.
It was time to return to the village.

The walk was a peaceful one as Ashley concentrated on the sounds of the trees, the bugs, and the gentle purring of the Bumble Kitties, who seemed to have overcome their laziness and were now following him like his own furry army. He had slung his guitar over his shoulder so he could walk with his hands in his pockets and found himself humming as he made his way home. His hands were still a bit stiff and it felt nice to have the guitar out of them but even now he found he just wanted to sit down and play. But he needed a rest, and so did the guitar. He had come to rely on it these many years, and on the power it commanded. As soon as anyone saw him with the guitar in his hands they knew who he was - he was *the boy who sang*. He was *the boy with the guitar*. He was both things but, who was he in a year, when he was eighteen and a man. Who would he be then? Would he be anyone then? Was he anyone now?

He laughed.

If he'd learned anything over these past years,

and especially over the past few days, he knew what Kelvin had felt like before he'd been made Archduke and had made the decisions that had lead him to become the man he'd later regret. It was fear, the fear of losing the power, the fame, and more than anything the love of the people that had lead both Ash and Kelvin down the same dead-end path. These were the same things that had lead the Great Council to pursue the boy. Without Ash, without someone to bring out the people, someone to bring out the money, the Council would lose its power, would lose its voice, and, in the end, would become as useless as the many laws they had created. Ash smiled at this thought and it was then that the sounds of music started to get louder and Ash slowed his pace. He still marveled at the power of the young boy's voice. His was certainly the voice of a child but there was a maturity to it, a wisdom in the way he shaped the song that made his talent so special. Many could sing, it was true, just as many people could do any sort of art, but finding the person that could take something and make it breathe, make it live, well, that was a rare thing indeed. Ash smiled and realized he'd stopped moving completely – the music had taken him for a moment. He shook his head to clear it and realized that he was at a bit of a crossroads – to the left was the home of his parents, to the right, the stage. The question became – was he meant to go to the stage, to speak to the boy, the people, and the Council?

Was he meant to tell everyone what he'd learned? What he'd experienced?
He thought a moment and yes, that would be a very good thing to do, an important thing.
It just wasn't a wise thing to do.

He started walking again and found himself before the door to his parent's home within twenty minutes. He knew that if he let himself, he'd wait out there in the spreading darkness until either his mother and father found him themselves, or he would wait out there all night, until he got the courage to knock. Before he had a chance to re-think things he knocked on the door and took a step back.

It was a long few moments as he waited there but he heard voices, had heard laughter, and so he knew someone was home, it was just a matter of whether or not his parents would want to see him. There was a commotion inside the house as dishes clanked together, as chairs were shifted, and suddenly the door swung wide and there before him was the most beautiful woman Ashley had ever seen. Her hair looked as if a rainbow had gotten entangled in it and she had a smile that almost gave off light. She was tall and thin and wore a small, simple crown atop her head and on her body she wore flowing emerald robes that reached to the floor. Ash had had everything he wanted to say worked out, had planned it all out on his walk back, but suddenly his tongue felt as if it had swollen and he seemed to have swallowed all his words accidentally.

"Ah, you must be Ashley then?"
Ash nodded, unsure who this was, how she knew him, and wondering why he was even there. He was struck silent by her beauty and the glow that seemed to come from her. He felt warm, as if he was sitting in the sun and that warmth made it hard to speak or think. Suddenly his father was at the door, laughing about something but his laughter stopped when he saw Ash and an awful feeling ran down Ashley's spine – what if his mother and father didn't *want* to see him. What if…

"Ashley? *Ashley?*" His father rushed forward and embraced him. All of the breath disappeared from his lungs and the warm feeling filled him again. Everything he'd had to say had left him and now all he wanted was to remain here, in his father's embrace, a place he hadn't known for months. His father pulled away and looked a little embarrassed as he took a step away from Ashley.

"Oh, oh my, please Queen Messy, excuse my rudeness, I got a little carried away. Ashley, this is the new Queen, I mean to say, this is *our* new Queen, Queen Messy."
Ash stood still a moment, unsure what to do but remembered his manners and bowed to the Queen.

"A, uh, a pleasure to meet you, my Queen." Messy smiled.

"Please, do me a favor and call me Messy, will ya? I have been trying to convince your mom and dad to do the same since we met yesterday and they just refuse to do it. It's driving me crazy, I have to tell you. So, I see you like music too."

Ash blushed, having forgotten the guitar on his back, and was shocked that even the Queen had heard of his singing, but it seems she had something else in mind as she pointed over his shoulder and he turned. There, behind him, were hundreds of Bumble Kitties who must have followed him back from the lake. He let out a laugh and shook his head.

"Ah, you laugh, you must know these kitties well then." Said Messy.

"Well, in a way, I suppose I do. They were quite a bother for a while but I finally appreciate them for what they are."

"Bumble Kitties are amazing animals Ash; it's rare to find them become so attached to someone, usually that only happens with people of extraordinary musical talent. The kitties themselves seem to have gotten a bad reputation over the years though as lazy little things that seem to lull people into being lazy themselves. And I suppose all of that is true, in a way, but truth is rarely as simple as that. Bumble Kitties aren't actually lazy at all. They live very simply and keep to themselves usually. The fact is that all the kitties really care about is music. Once they find a place where there is music, pure music, then they make their home there. They are muses, they live to help people make and appreciate music. It's said they were the pets of the Song Mothers of old, which is why they are still so attached to music. It's what makes them happy. A lot of people miss it but if you listen closely, each bumble-kitty's purr is completely unique. Each one of them has their own special purr, and in that purr, when it combines with another kitty's purr is music. Not a song perhaps, but the beginnings of a song. If you can find the right tune the Bumble Kitties will purr together and create the most beautiful song you could ever imagine accompanying you. If you hear just one of the kitties though, or the purring without anything to inspire it, well, it will put you to sleep better than anything around. It's not their faults but, well, their purr *is* very relaxing. We don't have a lot of the kitties on our side of the Kingdom, which I am working to change, but as we got closer to this area I remembered what your father had told me about you and it all became clear – I knew why we didn't have Bumble Kitties. It was because of you." Ashley blushed again.

"Me?"

"Why, there are not many people like you across the lands, Ashley Pickles, someone who creates such beautiful music and shares it with the people. Imagine my shock when I learned that there were *two* of you living so close to one another."

"You mean Glen, the boy who sings yonder?" Ash pointed towards where the stage was set up.

"I do indeed but I have been going on and on and on and I haven't even let you say hello to your mother. I would imagine that you have a lot to say to one another. How about I sneak off to watch Glen sing and you and I can talk some more tomorrow. Is that OK with you? I might try to have a word with him tonight as well, if I have time."

"If you have time?" Ash's father asked her.

"Well, I think I need to speak to some people about how things are being done around here. After our talk, Mr. Pickles, after what I see happening here, and what I have heard from the other rulers of the lands, well, I think some changes need to be made here in the Dark Lands. A *lot* of changes need to be made. I believe I have a Council to disband and some new people to put into place. And I mean what I said, I want your help with. But, for now, I bid you all good night.”

With that, Queen Messy and her entourage of three (an older man and two young women) left Ashley and his family without another word and headed towards the stage and the crowd. It was strange to see the Bumble Kitties flutter out of the way of the Queen as she walked through them, almost as if they knew who she was, and after what he'd learned, he believed it. As soon as she had passed them though, they returned to where they had been and looked back at Ashley and his family.

“Your mom made some soup, Ash, so why don't you come in here and have some dinner with us and we can catch up on things.”
“

“I'd really like that dad.” Ash replied, smiling.

“I mean, unless you'd rather stay out here all evening with your new friends.”

Ash laughed and hugged his father again. It seemed like months since he'd had dinner with his family and it was a very long time indeed before the smile left his face.

Mr. and Mrs. Pickles had heard the stories of

the new Queen as soon as they left the Dark Lands and how she was so special and different. It was surprising to them that they'd heard so little of her over the past few years, especially since she'd become such a popular figure in recent weeks but then again, they got very little news from the outside world in the Dark Lands, which was how the Council had wanted things. They heard though, on their travels, about her Meep Sheep, and about the path she took in choosing to become Queen and it only made the Pickles want to meet her all the more. After the coronation, and their first run-in with the famed Meep Sheep, Mr. and Mrs. Pickles inquired about a meeting with the Queen. They hadn't expected to be able to see her, with her just being made Queen and all but they had seen their lands become even darker since the death of the Archduke, and they had to do something. It had broken their hearts to see how his death had affected Ashley and now that he had his performing he seemed even more distant and lost than ever. After the coronation they made their way through the crowd of people and managed to find one of the aids to the Queen and told the woman where they were from and that they wanted to see the Queen and they were then told to wait in the Golden Plaza near the lake and she would bring word about when they'd be able to see the Queen. Mr. and Mrs. Pickles had done as they were told, happy to spend as much time in the Royal Citadel as possible, even if they didn't get to meet the Queen.

They had never seen so much sun in all their lives and to see the many creatures of the Kingdom roaming free took their breath away, laughing as they even saw a Smoochapotamus, a great pink beast that only came out at dawn to eat the flowers, its bites looking like kisses. They were wondering whether they might be able to rent a tent for the night out with the other people from the realm when came a sound behind them and when they turned there she was, the Queen, dressed in a simple dress and with her long, colorful hair pulled back beneath her crown. They stood quickly and she introduced herself to the Pickles and the three of them spent the next three hours talking about Ashley, the Dark Lands, and about Messy and her mother Anamare, the former Queen. It was Queen Messy that decided, after their talk, that she needed to start touring the other lands of the realm to see how things were going and that the best place to begin would be the Dark Lands, which was near to the Great Thicket, which was a vast wall of briars and trees that no one from the Lands of Man had ever crossed and which was where some believed the world ended. Mr. and Mrs. Pickles were shocked to hear that they were to be accompanied home by the newly crowned Queen but were even more stunned when her advisors agreed with the Queen's decision and made the preparations.

The troupe was off the next day and the Pickles

had scarcely met anyone as vibrant and hopeful as their young Queen. Queen Messy had never really had a chance to see the rest of the Kingdom as a young woman and each new village the group passed through was an exciting new world that never ceased to amaze her. The more she heard about the Dark Lands though, the more Messy realized that things didn't need to just change there, but they needed to change everywhere. If there was one thing her mother had told her, it was that yesterday was a promise, today a gift, and tomorrow a hope. It was Messy's job to keep that hope alive.

Back in the village a new day dawned.

When Ashley woke the next day he woke in his childhood bed, surrounded by his mother and father and embraced by love. He had had such dreams as he'd never had before. The dreams showed the Archduke, Kelvin, surrounded by blue light and the sweet sound of music and he was smiling, there in the middle of it, but behind him was a great, dark wall of brambles and trees. It was there that he was meant to go, the Thicket, where the world ended, and where music was swallowed up whole. When Ash awoke he woke knowing he'd turned a corner, he'd begun down a different path, but, that didn't make things any easier.

All through breakfast he found himself looking out the window of the cottage towards the stage and where he knew he must go. When it was finally time, he took his guitar, hugged his mother and father goodbye and left their house, only to be greeted by the waiting Bumble Kitties. It seemed they knew what he needed to do as well. Off in the distance he saw people filling the seats around the stage and he thought he saw Queen Messy and her entourage speaking to Glen and the Council, and the Council looked a bit ill from what the Queen was telling them. He smiled. It seems he wasn't the only one that had taken a new path, or at least, would be on a new path. Things were going to change, that was for sure.

Ash found himself at the crossroads again and stopped. To the left were the stage and an awaiting audience. To the right were the tree and the lake. He looked over his shoulder and saw that his companions were ready for a trip. A real trip. He cleared his throat and started singing, at first softly, and then the song pushed its way out of him and he could contain it no longer. As soon as they heard the song, the Bumble Kitties all rose into the air and started their melodic purring and suddenly Ash's song had an accompaniment more beautiful than even he could believe.

And they were off.

Ash and the Bumble Kitties traveled not to the left,

nor to the right, but forged a new path between the two, through thick grasses and weeds and towards a village called Morrow where he had heard they had not heard music in a great many years. A village, it seemed, that had banned music out of fear of its power. This seemed like the perfect place to start. It was one of the last villages before the Great Thicket and was the place he was to meet the Queen in a month's time, an agreement they made through notes early in the dawn when Ash revealed his plan to her. He had sent her a message in the night, to which she had replied, and in these messages were the beginnings of a plan, not just for them, but everyone. A lot of things were going to change, but first, the change had to happen in Ash, and he wasn't afraid, as he left the only home he had known. No, it wasn't fear he felt, but excitement.

There was nothing to fear.

Not when there is music and love.

Music was everywhere.

Wherever he looked, wherever he was, and whatever he did, music was there, waiting for him like a friend. And Ashley Pickles was going on this journey surrounded with music and friends, and the knowledge that things were about to change.

For everyone.

He smiled and began another song.

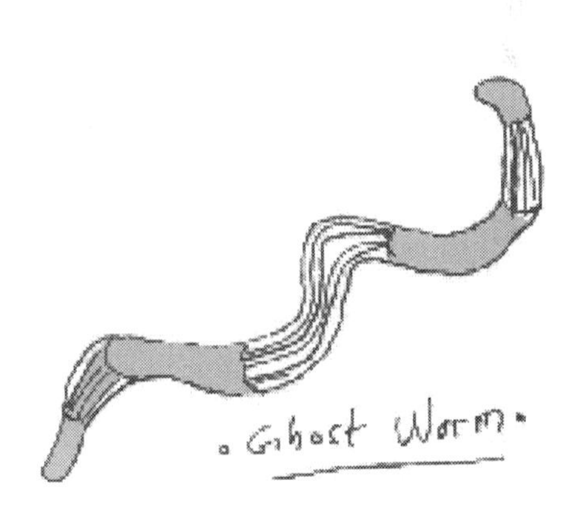
Ghost Worm

On a Day

essy stood near the water and let it lap at her bare feet.

It had been so long since she had been alone with herself and her thoughts that it was easy to forget the simple beauty of silence.

The trees whispered to her and she closed her eyes and smiled.

Off in the distance she heard the buzzing of a Bumble Kitty, beyond that a fluttering of a Meep Sheep, and further away, laughter.

Laughter.

All the time, all the exhaustion, all the tears, it was all worth it for that sound.

Everything was worth it for that.

The Queen opened her eyes and saw, in the distance, the balloons and tent peaks of a nearby fair. Perhaps she'd visit it on her way through as she headed towards the Great Thicket on the edge of her Kingdom.

Her friend Ashley Pickles was already on his way there but she was in no hurry to hasten towards the darkness. No rush to face the darkness to come.

It was not fear that held her here, up to her knees in the cool water of a small pond with her dress flowing and becoming one with the water, no, it wasn't fear, it was joy.

This moment, this one moment alone, this was hers, and hers alone.

Whatever happened next, here, in this moment, she

was pure, she was free. She was just Messy, not the Queen, not a Mistress of Magic, not anything but a young woman enjoying the day and to her, that's what made it so beautiful.
It didn't matter what she did next, or what might happen next, what mattered was she believed in herself, and the rest, the rest would come as it would. She smiled to herself and took a deep breath of the air, so full of the scent of flowers and Spring-time, and she smiled and stepped from the pond.
She was ready to go.

Willow-wilf

Manda and the Pandas

manda was mad.

No, she was *furious.*

She looked out into the cold, dark night and saw nothing but green grass and green trees and green, green, green.

This was ridiculous.

It was Christmas Eve and there was no snow in sight. Not a bit, not an inch, there was not even a glimpse of any sort of snow anywhere and it didn't look as if that was going to change anytime soon, and that was just ridiculous.

Welcome to Willow Falls, the smallest province in the Kingdom of Man and a place where you could have snow every day for a year and then have three weeks of sunlight with no night in sight. This sort of weather kept things interesting, to say the least, but it didn't make things easy if you wanted to make plans. Amanda had been working on assignment taking pictures for the *Kingdom Times* for the past three weeks, covering the first national tour of the newly crowned Queen Messy and had been looking forward to her winter vacation. Winter was the time of the Renewal Festival which was a time of family and friends and where people would decorate their homes to give thanks to the gods of old, the gods of new, and to all the magic that made their world possible. For Amanda, the Renewal Festival meant that she'd get a much needed week off to see her boyfriend, her family, and to spend time with her dog. Ah, but things weren't working out the way she'd hoped, not in the least.

None of this was to say she hadn't enjoyed her tour, and she'd taken advantage of her travels with the Queen and her small entourage and had done some shopping in the more exotic shops and had gotten some gifts that really seemed to speak to the people she was buying them for. She was proudest of the Burping Bumberbash, which her mother was bound to love. She loved this time of year and as the days turned colder, her mind turned more and more to Renewal Eve and thoughts of her loved ones. All across the lands snow was beginning to fall, getting Manda giddy with excitement over the coming holidays. It seemed that everyone was getting into the spirit of things too as Messy herself had come to Amanda's room as she was packing to bring her a special gift. The Queen had been much impressed with the talent of the young photographer and wanted to give her a gift that she might get some use from. Messy had gotten some clay from the village of Perrian, a place known for its fine potters and sculptors, and had made a simple enough looking bowl but one which, when it was filled with water, became something very powerful when the time was right.

Amanda didn't quite understand why it was that Queen Messy was giving her this bowl which, though pretty and all was an odd sort of gift, but she took it, thanked her highness, and packed it away. Amanda hurried so she could make it in time to the vanneroo she had rented. The driver seemed delighted though to be surrounded by the Queen and her aides and didn't mind that Amanda was so late and even helped her with her bag. Content that she was going to have the sort of Renewal Festival her boyfriend always told her about, and which she'd heard tell of in the songs that people sang on their tour, Amanda fell into a deep sleep and dreamed.

In her dreams Manda was with her friends, family, and boyfriend, sitting around the great, magical flame that would be conjured for all to tell stories around and to share the things they'd seen and done since the last time everyone had met. It felt good to be with the people she loved. When the stories were done the old songs were sung and the presents were exchanged. It was a wonderful dream but like many dreams, it ended too soon, this time due to the driver as he shook her awake.

"We're here Miss, we're here in Willow Falls."

Amanda smiled and stretched inside the cab of the vaneroo as she got her backpack and slung it over her shoulder. The driver stood aside and Amanda

stepped out into what she expected to be snow. When there was no corresponding crunch to her step she looked down and saw grass, and beyond that was more grass, and grass, and grass, and grass. Everything here was green.
Winter hadn't even made it yet and festival was only a day away.
Amanda's heart sank.
She didn't see the driver as he took her bag off of the vaneroo and didn't hear him as he bid her a happy festival and didn't notice at all when he drove off into the night.
All Amanda knew was that it was time for Renewal and there was no snow in sight.

Every story Amanda had ever heard about the festival told about how beautiful the snow was, and how it made everything seem so perfect. This was the first time she'd be celebrating the Renewal with anyone other than her mother and dog and realizing that she wasn't going to have snow for her first Renewal with her boyfriend brought tears to her eyes. Manda made her way home from the station and saw that her message globe was blinking with messages but ignored it. She didn't want anyone to know she was home yet. She had a day, a day to make things right, to make it snow, and whatever it took, she was going to do it.

Amanda dropped onto her couch and her dog

nuzzled up alongside her and put his head in her lap, seeming to know she was sad. She petted him and he climbed up onto the couch with her, and as they both lay there, but her mind was somewhere else.

She spent many hours thinking about her problem, how she should solve it and it was late when Amanda decided she had a place to start, somewhere she might find an answer, but as much as she wanted to get something done, she knew she had to get some rest.
So she slept.
And she dreamt.
And in her dreams it snowed.

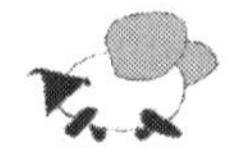

The next morning Amanda got up early and dressed quickly then made her way to the office of the village elder. Her name was Iridor and she had inherited her mantle from her brother, who had been lost in a long ago battle during the Great War. She had been elder for a great many year and she had become the voice of reason in the village and knew many of the old magics, and was said to have been the daughter of a Song Mother. Amanda came to Iridor to ask her one question and one question only – *why?*
That was all it took Iridor because she had seen Amanda coming to her in a Seeing Stone and had

heard similar questions from the others in village.
Why wasn't it snowing, they all asked.
Why?

"It is the Pandas, my dear. You see, they have always been jealous of our Renewal Festival and the things we share with one another in this time. They have no such customs and they resent that we do." Amanda frowned.

"But Iridor, how can they do this? What power do they have over the elements? How can they stop it from snowing?"

"Their elder possesses the Winter globe, one of the four globes the Narcissan kings had made for them so they might control the weather. The other three, Spring, Summer, and Fall, are said to be lost, perhaps within the Great Thicket, but the Winter globe came into the possession of the Pandas some time ago and it seems they've decided to finally use it."

"But what can we do to make them stop this? How do we convince them that this is wrong?" Manda asked.

"I would imagine that if the new Queen were too…"

"There is no time for that though, madam Iridor.

Tonight is Renewal Eve."
"Then I guess for this year, there will be no snow. I am sorry child. I wish there was more I could do. I can do a great many things, work much magic, but to conjure false snow on the Renewal Eve is forbidden, I am afraid."

Amanda's frown deepened as she thought, but beneath that frown, far beneath it, there laid a smile waiting to be born.

Amanda had done a story about the Panda Kingdom the previous year, when a new trade accord had been reached where the Pandas would be given bamboo from the distant lands of the Kingdom and the Pandas would provide protection spells to ward off anything that might emerge from the Great Thicket. Relations between Pandas and the people of the Kingdom had always been strained but it appeared that things were starting to get better, and then this happened. What Amanda couldn't understand though was why they had only halted the snow in this area, and not across the Kingdom. Maybe it was a warning. She wasn't sure but she intended to find out. She packed her things, even the bowl she'd been given by the queen so she might have something to eat and drink from, and headed for the lands of the Pandas. It was a day's journey, at least, but Amanda had learned a spell from one of the queen's aides that would transport her to within a mile of wherever she wished to go. It took you no closer because it was a spell that had been used during the times of war and was meant to aid spies, but it had come in handy with the royal family when they needed to be somewhere very quickly. The spell was such that you could only use it in a time of need, otherwise you might be sent somewhere far from where you intended to go so it was not a spell to use lightly. So, making sure her pack was closed and ready, she closed her eyes, bowed her head and uttered the words she'd been told and suddenly she was gone, her dog left to wonder where she'd gone to as he sniffed for any sign of her.

The Kingdom of the Pandas was a modest area set upon rolling hills and full of many caves. This place had been abandoned by the humans after the wars due to its distinction as the location of a slave camp but the Pandas felt no such disdain for the area and found it to suit their needs perfectly. Manda stretched upon arrival and looked around to find a world coated in white. Amanda's anger grew suddenly as she looked out across the land and saw that it had snowed here and worse, she could see that there was a Renewal Festival fire off in the distance, in the city. She pulled her coat tight around her and was about to start moving towards the fire when a loud growl stopped her. She spun to her left and saw that a great red Panda, a War Panda, was standing nearby, hiding in the shade of a tree. It was dark here, the sun trapped behind clouds, and the shadows made the Panda seem all the more terrifying as it stood on its hind legs watching her.

"What do you want here, little girl?"

"I come to see the elder. I want to speak to them."

"And what would a human have to say to the Great Loof?"

"I have come to speak to, uh, the Great Loof about the snow, and why my village doesn't have any."

"Ah, so it worked then, the Great One will be pleased to hear that. Very pleased indeed. Well, it seems as if you may indeed have something interesting to tell the Great Loof after all. Follow me, but don't try to run off or I'll have to come get you, and you won't like that much at all."

Amanda nodded and did as she was told, following the great red Panda as it dropped onto all fours and waddled its way through the snow and towards the fire. She wasn't sure what she'd hoped to gain by coming here, she was no dignitary, she was no Queen, but she had to try. Perhaps if she could just show them how important this festival was, perhaps she could convince them to give back the snow. The two of them walked in silence through the snow, both lost in thought, the only sound the crunching of the snow beneath their feet. Amanda marveled at the Panda capital city as they entered it. It was built of simple enough things – wood, leaves, and dirt – but it was beautiful, and looked so natural she would have thought these structures had always been here. It felt, she realized, as if the land was clean, was pure again, and that the war had never been here at all. She'd been here once before, with her mother when she was a girl, to see the place her father had died, and the place had given her the creeps. Now though, now it felt, well, it felt good. She smiled.

"What are you smiling at, girl?" Asked the Panda.

"How did, oh, never mind, I was just smiling at how beautiful your city is."

"Yes, yes, it is. Thank you. It took a great many years and many hundreds of hours of work but we did it. Our kind has wandered these lands since the Dim Days, never having a real home of our own since we left the Thicket before your kind was even here, but after all those years of wandering we finally have a home. We have a place to call our own. That is a very important thing to us, but you might not understand."

"Oh, I think I can appreciate that."
"Maybe you can, girl, maybe you can."

"Can you just call me Amanda, or even Manda, if you don't mind? That's my name."

"So be it, Amanda. And you may call me Alloos, though, you won't need to call me anything any longer for we have arrived. Welcome to the center of Ooon, our capital city, and the home of the Great Loof."

As Alloos spoke several more red Pandas appeared, spears slung over their broad backs, and their eyes narrowed to slits as they watched Amanda. Alloos spoke to them in pandese and the others backed off but followed. As they entered the center of the city Amanda was shocked to see hundreds upon hundreds of Pandas, and, she was surprised to see, not just the red war Pandas or the black and white Pandas, but Pandas of every type and color she might imagine. There were even some Pandas in the far back of the crowd, which towered over all others and which wore great helmets on their heads, their coloring changing from moment to moment. Those must be the great war pandas that were so rarely seen but went out only when battle was imminent. Amanda was so caught up in all she was seeing that she almost missed her introduction to the Great Loof, who was bore the same ability as the color

changing Pandas in the distance, though he was far smaller than they were. He truly took her breath away when she saw him.
She knelt before him, feeling that was what was expected of her.

"What do you wish of me, human? What business do we have?"
Alloos spoke up but was told to let Amanda explain herself.

"I have come, O, Great Loof to ask you if you might return winter to my village tonight."

"Ah, so my stone worked; good. Good. And so you say then that there is no snow at all in the Kingdom of Man?"

"No, no it is just my own village that is without snow."

"Pity. I shall have to work on that. I am the first to use the winter stone for a great many years so it may need some time to get working properly."

"But why on earth did you do it, Great Loof?"

"It was, a lesson I suppose. It was our way of reminding you that there are others in this world, others who might like the pleasure of such things as the Renewal Festival. Others that should be considered and not ignored. It was a childish trick, but it did get your attention, did it not?"

"It did sir but, I don't understand. Why would you want to ruin something that is so sacred and important to so many of us merely because you cannot take part in it yourselves?"

"Because, my child, we were never invited *to* take part in the festivities. We realize that relations have been strained for a great many years but that doesn't mean that we don't wish that to end. Our people were the first to celebrate the Renewal Festival in a time before any of your ancestors walked these lands, but we lost our traditions during the wars and it has taken a great many years to get those traditions back. By the time we were ready to reclaim the festival though, we found that your kind had already taken it from us. Well, we have decided we want the festival back."

Amanda was silent then, unsure what to do. She hadn't anticipated this reaction and didn't know what to say. What she did know is she was hot, was burning up in fact, despite the cold and snow, and the heat seemed to be coming from her backpack. She tried to put this out of her mind and spoke again.

"But Great Loof, why can we not share this

tradition? My people obviously saw something special, something that your kind also saw, and now we have to opportunity to change the future, to move away from the pain we have shared, and to walk together into tomorrow."

"These are fine things to say but they are words, and words from but one of your kind. We are not much for words but actions, and the actions of your people have shown us nothing of friendship. I think we are done, Alloos will see you get back to your land safely."

There was some movement amidst the Pandas and much whispering. Her heart sank - she had failed. The red Panda moved forward again, away from his place beside the large throne made of wood that Loof sat upon, and towards Amanda. She had nothing to do but to follow Alloos and to go home. She'd have to make the best of the holiday that she could. It just seemed as if she'd been so close, so close to convincing them. She glanced over to her left and saw two young Pandas sitting together, watching her. These Pandas were passing a bowl back and forth and drinking something from it that steamed. As they shared the bowl they would bow their heads together and bump them as the bowl passed between them in what had to be a gesture of friendship.
Suddenly she had it.

Amanda dropped to her knees, forcing Alloos to stop abruptly behind her, which drew all attention back to the two of them. There was more whispering and rustling and the Great Loof rumbled with anger. Amanda tried to put all of this out of mind and pulled her clothes and food from the backpack and then there it was. As soon as she had it the bowl was burning in her hands and glowing, as if had been trying to tell her the answer all along. The bowl!

"What is the meaning of this? How dare you interrupt our celebration yet again? We have had our words, and now, I ask you to leave before you anger my people further." Growled the Great Loof.

Amanda pulled the bowl out of the bag and then grabbed a small flask she had of Willow Mead, the drink her village was known for and something she hoped might work to her favor. She rose and turned back to face Loof.

"O, Great Loof, forgive me my interruption. I came to you, on the eve of the Renewal Festival, and I didn't offer you a drink of Mead from my home. Please accept my deepest apologies and, if you will, would you share a drink with me?"

Amanda knelt again and took a deep drink of the mead and felt its warmth light a fire within her.

Beside her now, Alloos was uncertain what to do. He didn't know whether to simply pick the girl up and carry her off, or if he should stand aside - he chose to stand aside. There was a sudden silence that fell heavy upon the city. The fire behind Loof roared and glimmered, casting shadows upon the faces of all the Pandas that surrounded her. She felt very small, and very weak, and as if she'd made a very big mistake.

After a few moments of silence there came a deep rumble from the Great Loof's belly that grew louder and deeper as it moved upward, echoing through the city and out over the land. The rumble made its way up, up, up and finally to Loof's mouth and out of it came a loud, thick laugh that shook the ground.

"Willow Mead, you say? I have always wanted to taste the sweetness of that mead. Always. And dear girl *my* always carries back a great many years. I will accept this drink, and gladly."

Amanda rose and hurried forward to Loof and knelt before him and held the bowl out to him. The bowl glowed brighter now and he tipped the drink back and drank deeply from it. As he drank the bowl's color turned from deep red to light blue. Loof finished his drink and wiped a paw across his mouth. His colors had stopped changing and he too was blue, his body light and around his eyes and face a much deeper blue.

"Finer mead, I have never tasted. Thank you for the drink and for the gift of friendship you have offered. I accept it, and offer my own."

The Great Loof leaned forward in his throne and motioned for Amanda to rise and come closer. She came to the foot of the throne and stood there, and as she stood Loof dipped his head forward and leaned into her, she smiled and did the same and their two heads touched gently. Around them a chorus of roars rang out through the hills and the festival began anew. Amanda and Loof were now just two more friends among many.

"What do you say, Amanda is it, if Alloos told me well, I return the snow to your village? It *is* the time of Renewal after all."

Amanda smiled and did something she wouldn't have dared to moments before and leaned forward and hugged one of great Loof's paws.

"Thank you, thank you so much. I can't wait to get back to my home to celebrate the festival with my family."

Loof was silent a moment then smiled to Amanda –

"Seeing that this is the first time our people will celebrating this great festival together, this important time for family and friends, what do you say you and your loved ones spend the Renewal with us, as our guests? I think you were right in what you said, it's time to walk towards the future together, and this can be our first step."

She hadn't meant to but Amanda started crying and hugged Loof again, and that was all the answer he needed. He picked up a beautiful blue stone from beside his throne and blew into it, and when he did, the stone glowed and grew transparent and within it a great many things began swirling and, to Amanda, they looked like snowflakes. That done, he called out for the largest of the Pandas to come forward. These were the last of the Panda-tar-too, and, like he, were beings of pure magic. It fell to them to help Amanda gather her family and return to the city safely, and this was a task they seemed to take great pride in.
In another moment Amanda was on the back of one of the Pandas and they were off, like whispers in the wind and flying and as they flew, Amanda felt the snow hitting her and they were like the best kisses she had ever had.
In the distance the bells rang out, and it was time, it was Renewal Eve, and soon she'd be with the people she loved, and with people she'd grow to love, and would be walking towards tomorrow.

The Meep Sheep

meepus sheepus

And there

Up in the sky

I saw a dream of Hope

And smiled

From

Darkness

Doubt

Despair

They came.

They are –

Sunshine

Laughter

Daffodils in rain.

I saw them in my heart and the shadows fell away.

And I smiled to see them

Knowing –

Had I eyes I could see them

Had I ears I could hear them

Had I heart I could hope

And had I *me*, I had *them*.

I dreamt of Hope and found my Meep Sheep.

They dreamt of me and Found their Home.

• water dragon •

• kumberboo •

No One and the Great Thicket

The old man was called No One to any that wished to ask but, being that none did, he was just No One, the keeper of the Great Thicket and the only person to have stepped foot into the wilds beyond the wall. The wall, such as it was, was much lower when he crossed it and he was much younger, younger even than one might ever imagine, he being older than one might believe, and that one trip over changed his life forever and always. Most of the stories, legends, and many of the myths about the Great Thicket began with him, a thing he wasn't terribly proud of but which was what it was. He had come back from there aged ten years, though he'd only been gone a few minutes. He was the only one though, the only one to cross the barrier and return and now, now he was the only one that stood to make sure not another soul went over again. Sure, some made it; some made it over the barrier which, by No One's hands had grown to twelve feet high from mountain to river, and those that did pass over the barrier never returned. There were some that said that there was a sort of paradise over that barrier, through the Thicket and beyond but No One, the old man who guarded the pass to the Great Thicket, believed different, and it was he that people believed. And so it was that No One, the oldest of all the peoples in the Kingdom of Man, guarded the way and blocked the path, but even he couldn't have imagined what he had yet to turn away.

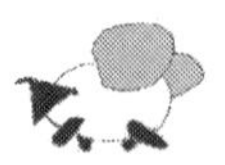

My but it was a beautiful day – the air was clear save for the passing of an errant Meep Sheep, the wind was warm, and the water was cool on a hot body. Ashley Pickles had been walking since dawn and now, at mid-day, it was time to take a dip in a secluded pond and to see what he had to eat for lunch. It had been three weeks now since he had left his family, his home, and his village and he had yet to meet up with the Queen, though he knew he was growing closer by the day. He could feel her sometimes as he walked, or rather, could feel the remnants of her warm magic in cool lands. Lately, he could also see her in his dreams. It was strange, these dreams, because he knew she shared them with him and it was in these dreams that they confided in one another, encouraged one another, and spurred each other onward. They had planned to meet in Morrow but she had been delayed in Ashley's home village and so he had pushed ahead without her, leaving behind him the seedlings of music that he hoped would bear rich fruit some day. As for he and Messy though, something was waiting for them up ahead and it drew them both, step by step, towards it. It was hard not to be fearful of what lay ahead but they knew that whatever happened, they had one another, and that was something. It wasn't love that bound them and entwined their dreams but friendship of the kind and rarity that few are ever lucky enough to find. It was this friendship that pushed them on through the rains, through the cold, and through gray lands that had not seen a smile in decades. Ashley, who, like Queen Messy, had never seen much of the Kingdom or lands beyond, would never have imagined there could be such sorrow as he was finding. It was as if the further from the center of the Kingdom, the home of the Queen and where the Great Court met, the darker the lands got. It was hard for Ashley, someone to whom laughter and song came so readily, to find people who didn't even know what music sounded like anymore, or that a smile could come so easily. Harder for Ashley though was the deep loneliness he felt on the road. His Bumble Kitty companions, once so great in number, had dwindled to but three, an orange tabby, a sandy brown cat, and a great black cat that seemed to sleep even as it was awake, its body so heavy and gait so slow. Despite the loss of the other kitties, who no doubt had found some tree or other that would make for a wonderful nap, Ashley still missed his parents, who were back in his home village, helping to support Glen, the young boy that had taken up as a singer in the area. The days were long, the nights longer, and it was a hard journey but whenever Ashley felt down he would find a shady tree, take off his shoes, pull his guitar from off of his back, and would start singing. In the end, no matter what difficulty there was, or what hardship, there was always the music.

The music, above all else, was his constant and never faltering friend.

A hundred miles away, and facing other, vastly different challenges, was Queen Messy who was on a tour of the lands she had become ruler of upon her eighteenth birthday. The intention had been to meet Ashley weeks earlier but the more she learned of her Kingdom, the more she realized that their meeting must wait, and that other business must be attended to first. She had learned much over these past months but the most important thing had been that there was a danger at the edge of her realm, a shadow in the form of the Great Thicket, a place no one had been to and returned for a great many years. As a girl she had heard tales of the place and it was the one thing her mother had feared, and for that alone the place held power over her.

As she had traveled with her entourage and a young reporter named Amanda who was covering this journey, the Queen had been asked time and again what she was going to do about the Thicket. At first she had simply told the people she would have her advisers look into it but, the more they looked into it, and the more *she* looked into it, the more she felt that this was not a problem that was going to go away. Sure, people were worried about the crops, about the weather, about their neighbors, and some were worried that stories of new creatures in the land were true but more than anything they worried about the Thicket, and what horrors it held just out of sight. It was in the the capital city of the Great Pandas, who were recent allies of the Queen thanks to the work of Miss Manda, that she made her mind up to do something about the Thicket. That even the pandas, such brave, and majestic people, would not speak about the Thicket said much to Messy. She had heard tales that they had come from the place once upon a time, heard it even from Manda herself, but this seemed more like a legend than anything else. Many a night Queen Messy sat up and stared deep into the darkness, watching the thunderbugs crashing into one another in the distance and setting off traces of lightning through the sky and lighting the world below. The dark weighed as heavy on Messy as the reality of the Thicket itself but at least the darkness could be held back by the light of the day, but the vast gloom of the grim forest was something that she would have to face, would have to explore, would have to tame, and it scared her. The only thought that held back that bit of darkness was the knowledge that she would not be alone. That friend Ash would be there with her, standing by her side. When it was said she was traveling to see the lands, and would be near the borders where so much trouble had been seen during the wars there were those among the panda tribe that had volunteered to accompany her to fight whatever lay ahead but, for now, Messy felt it best to take this battle alone. She told the pandas, proud peoples that they were, that this was not a time for war, a time for aggression, but a time for diplomacy, and a time for her, as Queen, to find what it was exactly that they were facing before any acts of aggression were made. And this all sounded reasonable enough to the pandas, and to their elders, who touched their heads with Messy as a sign of trust and acceptance, but Manda, she felt differently. She had been with the Queen long enough to know when she was scared and she saw it now in everything Messy was doing, and this concerned her deeply.

"Queen, may I have a word with you?" Asked Manda as the entourage moved away from the panda city.

"You know you can Manda. Ask me anything you'd like. To you, I am an open book."

"It's about the Thicket and the pandas. They are brave, to the last of them, and I know that they trust you and would travel with you, protect you to the end if this were about the borderlands, about the Outer Realm, but it isn't, is it? You are going to the Thicket and know that should you ask them, if you asked them, they would refuse to come. Not out of fear but because they know things about the place. I have asked them, and they will not say what they know, good or bad, but if such as they came from there, can it be so awful a place? They are afraid, but I do not think it is of the Thicket but of what you will find there." But Manda, knowing the Queen well, saw in the eyebrow that slowly rose, that this was a conversation that was over before it had begun.

"I noticed that myself Manda. Yes, I agree, the pandas, a great people of these lands, are still distrustful of we humans and of our affairs, such as the Thicket. That is why I did not accept their offer of help. Until I know that there *is* a problem, in the Thicket or elsewhere, I do not want to look like an army. And as I think on all this, I think to even travel with more than myself may be a waste of resources. You have accomplished so much in your time here, in Ooon, I think it's best if you stayed on with them, as my, uh, as my envoy. They seem to trust you and I think it would be good for the rest of the Kingdom to read about their culture and people, so they can get better accustomed to these new friends of ours. We have much time to make up for, don't you agree?"

Manda knew when she was being lied to but, this time, this time it seemed not that she was being told a lie but as if the Queen, who was lying to herself. Her heart sank then, knowing that, whatever was to come, whatever was going to happen, she would not be there for it, and it wasn't the journalist in her that was saddened but the friend. She nodded slowly to her Queen and looked back over her shoulder a moment before looking to the Queen again.

"I suppose you are right. I can keep in touch with my family and boyfriend via courier and can send in my stories via Sound Stone, so if that is your wish, then I will stay until you tell me it is time to leave."

"Good. I am glad you see the importance of this assignment. In these times, where the shadows are gathering around us, we need to all be together to fight it back. You're doing important work Manda, keep it up." Messy smiled to Manda and gave her a quick hug before moving to speak to the head of her entourage. The man, Lias frowned deeply as she spoke to him, started to argue with the Queen then snapped his mouth shut when she gave him a look all Queens, and any mother, had been able to command, and that was the end of the discussion. The Queen moved away then to the automagical carriage that was at the head of the small parade, gave a wave to everyone before getting in, and was gone. Lias came up to Manda and put his hand out to her. She looked at his hand a moment, then a moment longer but when he cleared his throat she realized he wanted her to shake it so she did as she was bidden.

"Miss Manda, I am Lias, head of the Queen's guard. It seems the Queen has decided that, that, well, the procession is to stay with you during your time with the pandas. She seems to think it'd be good for us to learn from their warriors and for us to share our training with them. Personally, I think it's insane to, well, well, she has told me that we are to accompany you back to the city. *All* of us."

Manda's mouth dropped open at this revelation.

"But, but how can, that, why…you're not going to do that, are you? I know she wanted to go out alone but I never thought you'd *let* her. You can't let her go off on her own."

"As she told me herself, she is the Queen, and this is her Kingdom. She feels she is safe here. And, if the worst should happen, if a problem should arise, we have agents all across the lands that are ready to strike at a moment's notice. This last she does not know, and I'd ask you not to alert her. I had people put into place before she set out on this *adventure* of hers and now it seems I was right to do it."

"But…" Was all Manda could muster.

"It is what it is, Miss. This is the will of the Queen and it's my job to serve that will. Now, if you'll take your bag and head back towards the city to alert them of our change in plans I'll speak to the rest of the entourage.

Manda did as she was asked, heart heavy, her stomach full of rocks and wondering if the Queen really had any idea what she was doing.

And in the carriage the Queen cried softly to herself, trying to stop but unable to so she hid her face in her hands. As soon as she had been away from her people she had stopped for a moment to collect herself, though that moment was taking longer than she had hoped. It was a bitter truth that revealed itself to her then that the greatest stories are those we never tell, and the worst lies are the ones we tell ourselves. Messy sat there, the world veiled in tears, then took a breath, wiped her face, and pressed the levers forward and the carriage began moving again, a small wagon full of provisions in tow behind it. The Queen looked up and saw the clouds pushing slowly across the sky. Suddenly a dark cloud erupted from between the others and it circled round and round and round then disappeared again, and Messy felt a chill as she watched it, unsure quite why. A moment later she heard a distant 'Meep' and smiled through her tears, as a friend, hearing her crying, was coming to cheer her up.
Far above though, a dark shaped moved amongst the clouds.

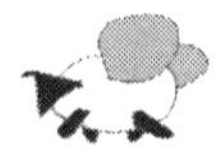

All across the Kingdom of Man the sun shined, and the people rejoiced. It was the Time of the Sun and all the snows had melted and there was a renewed alliance with the Pandas, and it was said that their Queen was headed towards the Great Thicket to find the truth about what lay beyond. The Great Thicket had become the boogeyman for many villages and villages in the Kingdom of Man because so little was known about it. Some said great monsters lay beyond the brambles, while others claimed it was the edge of the world and beyond was nothingness, a great black place where nothing existed. The Thicket was a place of great mystery and had become the object of many young people's obsessions as they journeyed out to conquer it, though all but a few wised up enough to become fearful, the others being scared off by No One, who watched the Thicket, and a few, a few disappeared altogether. Once in a while someone would set out the idea that perhaps there was something good and kind beyond the Thicket but they were usually shouted down as mad.

You see, the Thicket was old, very old, and went back to the days before the first Mistress of Magic, to the days of the War Kings and the Grim Times, when the sun was blacked out by the smoke and thunder of combat. As old as the Thicket was, it had been planted. It was not natural. This much was known. It was said that a wizard, a servant of the King Edgewood, had created the Thicket as a barrier so that the King and his family could escape the war before it was too late. It was also said that when the family entered the new Kingdom something came with them, something from the war, and that it killed the family and was what lived in that land now. These things waited, patient and hungry and hoping the Thicket might one day fall so they could be loosed on the world again.

There had been explorers and people who had dared to brave the region nearest the Thicket but none were heard from again and were assumed dead. Even old generals, who had been the remnants of the lands before the Mistresses of Magic came to power, would head there with their armies and would disappear, never to be seen or heard from again. The one survivor was the old man named simply No One, who refused to speak to anyone and who kept a small cottage at the edge of the wood. Once, in the era of Mistress Lariadora, a young girl had dared to try to burn the Thicket, a dark rage unleashing in her and onto the woods, and much of the wood was lost, but the Mistress found out what was happening and quickly cast a spell that re-grew the Thicket and put out the flames. Lariadora was the last of the Mistresses to see the wooded areas. The girl was cast out of the Kingdom, a rare occurrence indeed, and

she wandered the world, going from one Kingdom to the next, but never finding a peace to her heart, and her name was Hush. Oh, there were other Kingdoms, and other places, but the relationships between them rarely went past the trade of goods, though it was rumored that the Mistress Messy had a plan to begin relationships with these other Kingdoms in time, but there was a more pressing concern before her. For now, she was on her quest for the truth about the Thicket and the people were eager for any news they could get. News on what had *really* happened was scarce though, and what the people heard they did not like –
The Queen had dismissed her entourage and was journeying alone now.
Beyond that, nothing was known.
Nothing.

And far, far away, Ashley Pickles was also alone, but lonely, he was not.

Ashley Pickles had been sleeping in a great open field under a full moon, the air warm and the sky empty. Even so far away from home he could almost smell his mother's cooking under these stars. The kitties had left him, for now, though he could hear them sleeping off in the distance, their purring snores giving him a fuzzy feeling that tickled his toes. With his guitar by his side he could almost hear music, but it wasn't his music but the music of Glen, the boy who had come to take his place in the village as its musician. What came to mind was the song he had been singing when Ash had left the village, something sad and sweet and familiar and strange, and something that moved him to tears then and to tears still, though now, the tears came because of where he was, how far he had come, and what was left to do. He wasn't scared about leaving his life behind but scared instead about the life that lay ahead of him. He had visited five villages so far, and each one he had done his best to given them back something they had lost – music. It was so long since the Song Mothers had gone, and the scars the war had left were still visible, even after so much time, and music, music had been gone, or taken by a woman that some called a witch. A monster. Ashley had been successful in four of the five villages so far, teaching them the song about his friend Kelvin, as well as others, but in one, one he had not been able to effect. One he had only stayed the night in and had been happy to leave. The village of Hiddion, which was said to have been the birthplace of the little girl who had tried to burn the Thicket down, the little girl some said who would go on to steal the music from the people eventually, village by village by village. The village had been cold, and distant, and there had been a shadow over everything there that no light could penetrate. They laughed as he sang,

and jeered as he tried to tell them tales of the new world that was being born as he spoke. They cared only to be left alone, and nothing more. So he gave them their wish and left that night, as they slept, and was happy to have escaped.
Now, far away from Hiddion, he still felt a chill from there as he stretched himself out and looked up into the sky. That chill left though as he saw a fluffy cloud pass over the moon and disappear, and a moment later heard the now familiar *meep* of a Meep Sheep. He closed his eyes and dreamed.

Mistress Messy also dreamed that night, asleep in the carriage and cold beneath a clouded moon. She had passed several villages, stopping in to two of them to speak to the people and to get supplies, and she was starting to see how hard this was all going to be. The villages had been polite, and courteous, and had shown her he respect due a Queen but none were happy to see her. They were suspicious, beneath the smiles, and she could tell that this was a place that was none too fond of the royal families that had ruled the Kingdom for so long. A little boy had come up to her as she was checking over the carriage and asked her in a whisper so others would not hear, if she was a witch. She had bent down and told him she didn't think so, but that he shouldn't be afraid of witches, that they were just people like him, and were many times just misunderstood. And the boy, tears in his eyes, asked her about the old lady, the old lady who had come and stolen the music from the village, and had turned some of the children into old people while she was here. Her name had been…but the boy had been swatted on the behind and ushered away before he could say more, his mother embarrassed but also angry at the woman who had only been there an hour and was already causing trouble. Messy had not stayed in these villages long, vowing to return as soon as she could but unsure she wanted to, or that they wanted her to return. This had been when her dreams had started to sour.

Far from her home, and the only world she had ever known, Messy shivered as she dreamed, and the evening's shadow cast itself long into her sleep. Messy was in the Great Woods and it was night. She was dressed in the gown and crown of her mother and the other Mistresses of Magic, items she had worn less than ten times, and even then only because it was expected. Messy had hated the formality of her position since before she had taken it but knew that it was expected, it was tradition, and so it was what she must do. She stood barefoot under the open arms of the trees of the wood, nervous and waiting. This was a revered and holy place for these were the trees that had seeded the entire world, and which lay at the heart of the Kingdom of Man.

From these trees the first castle had been built, and then came the village, and the first wall that kept out the last War King, came from these trees. These trees were the Motherwood of all the Kingdom which Messy ruled over, and it was here where the Queens would retire in peace once their rule was over. Messy had never seen the Great Woods before, this place being off limits to incoming or current Queens. She had heard from Mr. Naysmith once that while you never saw the Queens of old here, you could feel their presence, and it was a warm, happy feeling, as if nothing could harm you. They became one with the woods and watched over things and guided the Mistresses to come after them. Messy did not feel that warmth and safety though, as she started walking through the woods. In fact, she felt watched and unsafe and she felt uncomfortable in her robes and crown, and would have preferred nothing more than to remove them if it were a Queenly thing to do. She stopped walking at an open space and wondered if there was anyone else here but her. She called out and got no reply. This had to be the Great Woods, it had to be with the trees as big as they were, but if that was where she was, where were the voices of the other Queens? Where was her mother? She called out again to no reply and felt a chill run down her spine.

She was not alone.

She was about to start walking again, running if

her legs would steady themselves and not let her fall over, but before she could a very warm hand fell onto her shoulder and a soft voice came – *there's nothing here. Everything is here.* Messy screamed and spun around only to see herself and then was suddenly awake, tears streaming down her face. The Queen didn't sleep any more that night, or much for many, many nights to come, the haunted look on her own face in that forest of her foremothers weighing heavy on her mind as she lay in the dark thereafter with those chilling words chasing after her until well after dawn.

And while much of the rest of the Kingdom of Man and all the other Kingdoms slept, there was another whose dreams were of some importance this night, a man named No One who dreamt of what the Great Thicket, where the darkness was alive, and dreamt of a young Queen who thought she was somewhere else, and that she was alone there, but who wasn't alone at all.
Not at all.

Ashley awoke in a better mood than he'd been in for weeks. He woke to a shining sun and to his three companions purring patiently at his feet and he was famished, not so much for food as for the journey. He was getting close to his destination, to the Thicket, but It was time to get back on the road. There were more villages ahead of him but he needed to hurry. Time was running out, though he didn't quite understand what that meant. He stood and stretched and looked out over the field he had slept in and saw it was barren and abandoned. It was dead, and from how dry the dirt was, it had been dead for a very long time. Ash's head tipped against his shoulder and he squinted as he looked out over the field and was confused. The night before he had seen this as a rich and beautiful land but, the grass lush and soft, and that was what had drawn him here for rest but under sunlight and not moonlight, it was barren. Ash knelt and ran his hand across the dirt and felt how dry it was. Ash frowned and stood up again. He looked out over the field and saw a small cottage near the edge and sitting in two chairs in front of it were two old men who were watching Ashley as he watched them. His hands started itching and he felt suddenly hot. Ash felt as if he should do something but wasn't sure what it was and his mood darkened. Ashley paced back and forth, his shadow stretching and covering the dirt then twisting as he changed direction and spreading out in another direction. He was lost in thought when all the sound suddenly drained from the world, the wind died, and it was as if there was nothing left but he and the three bumble kitties, which had begun to purr in unison. Ash looked down at the kitties and saw they were looking up at him, sitting in the dirt and watching him as if he was expected to do something. But what?

He felt as if he was on fire, his hands itching, and it was like there was a voice calling to him, telling him what to do but he just couldn't make out...

It hit him like love and he suddenly knew what to do. Without thinking he bent down and picked his guitar up and held it in his humming hands and felt the heat run from them down into the guitar and then they started to play. He had never had something like this happen before, where his hands seemed to become possessed with the music. And there it came, music he had never heard before, had never imagined before, but which had been in him, in his hands, waiting for the moment and, with the help of his companions, out it came.

And what a song.

It was a song that was slow and meandering but which intensified and became a chant, a spell, a demand for the ground to release the seeds that lay dormant in its skin. It was a green song, that called to the dirt, to the air, to the sun, and to the water, and asked for all of these things to work together to free the seeds. The ground seemed to take on the heat of the song and beneath his feet he felt something moving. On he played and the song was lost in the hurried movement of his fingers then reappeared again as the song slowed and all over the field buds began to break the soil and took in the air of the day. The kitties rose and their purring intensified as well and their singing, and the singing of the guitar, were as one and Ashley was lost to all of it save for the song and when he was done, his hands aching and shaking and twitching with the music he looked up and saw the old were standing in the field now too. Ash started to move towards the men, to apologize for his behavior but as he took a step he felt something striking his leg, he ignored it and took another step and got more of the same. Thinking that the kitties were under foot again he looked down to tell them to shoo but instead of the kitties he saw that crops had risen from the ground. Ashley looked across the land and saw that crops had risen everywhere, for acres and acres. Ashley looked down at his hands as if they were not his own and was still.

Was this his path?

Was this the way?

One of the men rushed to him with the speed of someone half his age and embraced Ash, his face wet with tears. A moment later the other man ran forward and did the same. Ash wasn't sure what to do so he stepped out of the grasp of the men and tried to speak.

"I just, I just needed to play that song. I need it to get out of me. I, I am so sorry..."

"And son, your song has set the ground free, just as it set our hearts free. For untold years we have been cursed. The songs left this land those great many years ago, when the Song Mother left us for the Great Wood and when she left, so did our joy. After she left the music slowly disappeared from the land, the air, and the water, and as it disappeared so did the people. Yours is the first song this land has heard in all those years. Your song has set this land free." One of the old men told Ashley, the taller of the two who wore a red handkerchief around his throat and a smile upon his lips.

"I don't even know if it *was* my song, that's the thing." Ash told the men, his hands still hot but the guitar even hotter.

"Oh, it was your song, yours and your friends' that is. But it was the ground that called you, that called for you to sing to it, if you can understand. And it was the magic of your melody that revived our land."
The shorter man cleared his throat and looked up at Ash, his eyes having been on the crops the entire conversation. Around his neck was a blue handkerchief.

"Son, ain't nothing as it seems it is. Nothing. That ground you thought was dead wasn't dead at all, it

was just sleeping. Like me and my brother here. How old do you think we are? Take a guess."
Ash looked from one man to the other and scratched his chin with his free hand and thought a moment before answering.

"Are you in your sixties, maybe"?
The men laughed, but it was a sad laugh, a bitter laugh. The shorter one answered for both men.

"Son, we were dead before you came here with your song, or might as well have been. We are thirty eight years old, the both of us. We're twins, of a sort, being cousins raised by the same woman and born the same month, and the Song Mother was our grandmother. We had already lost our mothers to illness the swept our land and the Song Mother raised us for a short time, but a time that made a great impact on us and when she left we were alone again. And when she finally left we aged more and more by the day until we are exactly what you see – old, old men. As you walk through our land you'll find a lot of people who have aged, and aged deep, due to the sorrow we all feel. We sometimes forget how important something as simple as music is, and how important a part it plays in our lives."

"But, but why didn't anyone else just, well, just sing? Or play?"
"Ah, because no one taught us, my friend, no one

taught us. We had all believed the Song Mother would remain here forever and so no one learned to play an instrument or to sing. None of us are blessed with the gift to create music, which, well, leaves a lot of work for you. Let's get to it, shall we?"

"But, but I, I can't I…" And Ash felt the pull of the ground, of the earth, and more than those the pull of these men who seemed to need him so much but there was also the pull of the Thicket, and his responsibility. He could return here when he was done but for now, for now…

"My boy, who ever said you had a choice?" The man with the red handkerchief was smiling but there wasn't humor there and Ash knew that, for now, he had no choice but to go with these men and to hope for the best, but it was hard to shake the uneasy feeling this all gave him.

The old men held their hands out to Ash, their skin already smoothing out and their backs suddenly a little straighter, and so Ash picked up his sack and guitar and shouldered them and took their hands. The three of them and their three kitty companions made their way through the valley and as they traveled Ashley began meeting the people and seeing the land he saw that yes, he had a lot of work to do indeed.

Elsewhere, Messy had work of her own to do. Work

just as important, but not quite as clear.

Messy woke from a slight nap even more exhausted than when she had gone to bed, several hours earlier. She lay in the gloom of the carriage wondering if there was a chance that it was still evening and whether she had some time to rest but found that despite the darkness, it must be well into the day, and knew this from the sounds of labor that came from just outside of where she rested. Messy gathered herself, dressed as comfortably and plainly as she was able, and prepared herself for another day. She crouched in front of the door to the carriage, dim light slipping in at the bottom of the door, the dreams of the night still clinging tightly to her. The woods, the Great Wood, where the Queens were called, and to the center trees, the grove of six, where they gathered, and then the surrounding areas where those that passed from this life entered, it was of these places she dreamt. Places she had longed to see but knew she was forbidden from seeing until it was her time to go. But on seeing the woods, being there, she wondered if she would ever care to return because she *had* been there, she knew she had, and, looking at the soles of her feet, could see she had gone somewhere in the night. She had always believed the Mother Wood was a place of peace and beauty, a place where all became known, but when she was there she felt so lost, so alone, yet as if she was being watched and as the first dream had ended she had felt a presence and had spun around quickly to see who it was and had only seen herself. A ghostly image of herself that looked scared and broken and older than her years. But the image of herself had wavered a moment and behind that image had been a man, an old man who was watching her with keen eyes but the dream was suddenly over and she fell from that dream into another.

The second dream, while simpler, struck even deeper to Messy's heart, and it left a cold spot in its wake that kept her kneeling at the door, fearful of what she would find beyond it.

In the second dream Messy was completely alone, standing in a great field of beautiful yellow flowers, and above her the sun was high, the clouds were white, and all around her was the warmth of a soft breeze. It was a perfect day. Messy heard a sound and looked up to see if it was one of her fluffy friends but instead of a Meep Sheep though she saw a dark shape moving in the sky like a shadow in the bright day and as soon as that shadow would enter then exit a cloud that cloud would turn dark and become a storm cloud, and one by one the shadow did this to all the clouds of the sky until the day turned to a stormy night and the air turned chill and damp. And with all the clouds turned black, the shape did a great, slow loop in the air, moving just like a Meep Sheep, and then it headed for the ground and as it neared her Messy realized with dawning horror that it *was* a Meep Sheep, but one that didn't bring joy but misery. This Meep Sheep was dark gray and had bright red eyes and on its head was yellowed horns, and the closer it came the colder the air got and Messy feared what would happen should it touch her. Just as she feared what would happen should she squeeze it.

"Why, you'd die, of course."

Messy turned and saw her own ghostly image standing beside her.

"But, but what is it?" Messy asked herself.

"Why, doesn't it look familiar to you? Hmm? I call it a Kreep Sheep. If you are at all like me, it will like you. They will all like you. Just…give them a little squeeze – you'll see."

The thing hovered a moment then landed beside Messy's double, her hair various shades of gray, all the colors gone from it somehow. When the strange sheep landed it turned its eyes on Messy. Suddenly Messy wanted nothing more than to kneel down and touch, to squeeze it, and seeming to sense this, her ghostly twin smiled at her with all her teeth showing.

But as she watched her, Messy's double wavered, as if made of water, and beneath the water, beneath the surface of the double's skin it looked like there was an old woman but then the image was gone as quickly as it had appeared.

Messy awoke just as she had started to reach out to the Kreep Sheep and she counted herself lucky she had awakened when she had and was thankful to be away from that awful place. Unsure she'd be able or desirous of sleep she sat with her legs pulled up to her chest and listened to the sounds of the wind in the trees and thought about her most recent trip to the sacred woods. She had fallen asleep, an hour later, and had been thankful for the empty darkness she had found then, though it gave her no rest and did not dispel her of the memory of the other dreams. And now it was day, and while she knew it was silly, she wondered what exactly was awaiting her outside her door. And as she crouched there, wondering what to do next, there was a loud knock at the door to the carriage and with the knock came a voice, weak and frail, asking if anyone was inside. Messy fell backward onto her bottom after the shock of the knock but took a breath and rose, opening the door to meet the day and whatever it held for her.

All through the night No One had had dark

dreams. Dreams darker than the usual nightmares he suffered out near the Great Thicket. These were dreams of two people – the first a young woman that had the station of royalty but not the presence, and in the other of a young man who was on a great quest for himself, not seeing how close he was to finding the very thing that was right before his nose. Both were on their way to him but either could lose their way if they were not careful so No One watched over them as best he could to make sure they were not lead astray. There were many things that wanted nothing more than the Thicket to either overrun the Kingdom of Man or to be destroyed completely and neither were the path that No One could allow to come to pass. The old man woke late enough for the night to be fading and early enough for the dawn to be asleep and after waking he lay in his bed, rubbing the aching joints of his hands as a soft rain fell outside. He heard the crashing of trees and a familiar whoop off beyond the Thicket and knew he was not the only one having bad dreams tonight, and not the only one concerned with what was to come.

All across the Kingdom of Man people were having bad dreams. A dark wind blew through the Kingdom and stirred shadows in the hearts of one and all and in those shadows lurked a bent form that sung a black song, a reaping song older than any Ash had ever known, older than anyone had known save the Great Witches that had come from beyond the Thicket so long ago. This song slipped into the hearts of the people of the land and when the people finally awoke the next morning there was one place many of them they blamed for their uneasy sleep, for their unhappiness, their poverty, their fear and the rest of the problems in their lives and that place was The Great Thicket. And behind that thought there was fire.

It would seem that of everyone in the Kingdom had bad dreams that long, dark night the village of Umpton was the only place that was free of that ill wind, and it was all because of Ashley Pickles and his music. It could certainly be said though that for the people of Umpton, after years and years of troubled sleep, they had earned at least one night of rest. One might also mention people tend to sleep better after a long night of celebration, which had indeed been what had happened the previous night. After freeing the two men of the affliction of their age Ashley was begged by the people of the village to work his magic for the rest of them, and how could he refuse – the crops were stunted, the waters were heavy, and the air had a sting in it that made his head swim.

As soon as Ash entered the village square he was shocked to see that everywhere he looked was gray – the houses, the shops, the streets, the people, and even their pets had a bleak gray tinge. In the center of the village everyone stood slumped near the barren well as Ash was lead in by the two men – who were cousins close enough to consider themselves brothers – who in the walk from their home had shed years like beads of sweat. On seeing the two men there was a gasp that issued from the people in the square that moved like a wave from person to person as they realized that Adle and Pan had been restored to their youth once more. For their part, the men played the part of village heroes very well, dancing from person to person to let them prod and poke them to prove that yes, they were indeed back to their real ages, though Ash never would have guessed they were as young as they appeared, but how do you argue against the truth before you? As all of this was going on Ashley marveled that there were no children to be seen. But how could there be no children in twenty years? That question itched and itched in Ash's mind until he could take it no longer and, seeing that Pan was free a moment, he took him gently by the arm and leaned close to inquire.

"Dear friend Pan, I don't mean to be rude but, well, are there no children here? How can that be?"

Pan frowned at the question and looked over at Adle, who was dancing in a circle, to the amusement of the crowd that was gathering.

"That is a question better left unasked but you deserve an answer, though a whispered one. When all of this happened my cousin and I were but children, though not the last of the village. There were children still for many years but they too aged before their time and it was a terror to see so after five years all children in the village save us were sent away from here, to live in the village of Merilee, the closest village to us, and ever after there was a ban on having children here. None have seen their children in a many a year, the thought that it be better their children believe they have gone to the Great Clearing rather than deal with the reality of what we had become. All of that was because of the awful infection of melancholy that had spread through the village and now, now that you are here…"
Pan smiled at Ash.

"Ashley, friend, if your magic can work on the rest of Umpton as it worked on Adle and I, well, well…" And tears welled up in the eyes of Ash's new friend and he knew what he had to do, though he was struck again by how strange it was that Pan and Adle seemed to look so old in their eyes yet so young of body. It was a question for later though as he had work to do.

Ash looked around him and saw his kitty companions were still with him, though they were on the edge of the village square, their backs arched as they watched the crowd. Ash pulled his guitar off his back and as soon as he held it he felt the heat of the ground beneath him again, the life in the ground waiting to be set free and his hands were itching to be at their work and just like last time the nervousness left him and his mind was calm and he began to play.

As soon as Ash began playing the day became filled with music and Ash opened his eyes and saw that the gray was bleeding out of the ground, the buildings, and even the people were getting their color back but just as Ashley was finding a path with the song a scream stopped him suddenly. All eyes turned to a wizened old woman who was sitting in the shade of a business where strange blankets were sold. The woman rose slowly and wavered a moment before gaining her balance, her eyes issuing a warning that no one should dare to offer her a hand to steady her. The woman grabbed the cane that had rested beside her seat and slowly made her way to Ashley, who felt his heartbeat bounding through his head. The woman looked far older than the rest of the people but it wasn't her wrinkles that told Ash this but her eyes, which were narrowed and shaded and spoke much of someone who trusts little and suspects much. It was clear she had much to say but she was patient and waited until she was only two feet from Ashley before she spoke, her voice slicing a clearing through the silence.

"How *dare* you bring that, that *noise* to this place? How *dare* you, **Ashley Pickles**? Oh yes, I know your name, boy. I know all about you. The air speaks much about you, and that new Queen, though what it has to say of her is far less flattering. Neither of you know what you are doing, or the consequences of what you do, but you will learn though. Believe me, you will learn. Do you think you can so easily undo what others of deep magic, *old* magic have done? You have no idea what this place is, or the curse it suffers, and for that you will pay. Just wait boy, just wait."

The old woman smiled a toothless grin at Ash and then straightened herself and there was an audible gasp as the woman rose to a height that was greater than Ashley by several inches. She looked no longer like an old woman but like something else that wanted to look human for the moment. The woman let out a hollow laugh and made her way out of the village square and the people could hear her laughter for several minutes after she was gone and afterward there was a long silence from the village square.

Ash was shaken. He had never had someone speak that way to him, or about him. He didn't understand what the woman was so angry about and it shook him. He also didn't like that he felt that somehow what she said was not a complete lie. That there was something wrong here that he wasn't seeing. Ash closed his eyes and all he could hear were her words, all he could smell was the scent of cinnamon that had hung around her, and all he could feel was the heat in the ground, demanding he take up the song again, but he wasn't sure he could. But really, was that all? Was there not something else, something deeper, darker, something...

"Ashley, Ash, please don't take the words of Lady Hush to heart. She has been here a great many years, before even the Mothers of Man stepped from the Great Woods, though that seems like a dandelion tale to think she is that old. She is a wanderer, and no more. You cannot take her black words to heart. What we know is she has always moved from village to village and with her came misery, and with her came sorrow. These came not because she spread them so much as because she clings to such darkness, as some are wont to. She came here just as the Song Mother left and many blamed Lady Hush for the death of the crops and the aging, and some still do blame her, though it isn't for us to lay that blame."

"I, I guess I just don't understand her fear of me. Her anger." Ash replied to Pan.

"Because you can bring joy to all of us, to this entire village and give it a new life and you can bring us the one thing she has never known."

"And what is that, brother Pan?" Ash asked.

"Hope." But, Ash wondered to himself, is hope all you want?

All that day and well into the night Ashley played, and played as he never had before, the singing in the ground spurring him on and keeping him at it even when the Bumble Kitties took much needed naps, though they had done little of the singing if one were honest. When Ash would start to think about stopping he would see the people in the crowd and they were cheering him on, pushing him on, and he kept playing, past the exhaustion and pain, and into the evening. And while he played the village *was* transformed, person by person, brick by brick, tree by tree, the village was changed. It was as if ashes had been blown from the petals of a flower after a terrible fire that had consumed everything but that last piece of beauty. Ash played until his arms were sleepy, his hands numb, and his fingers bloody, he played until he could play no more and he finally collapsed in a heap beside the fountain. As soon as he stopped the people stopped dancing, stopped singing, and stopped talking and all eyes fell to him. He lay against the fountain, his breath coming in gasps and his hands aching. It was a good ache, a happy ache, but he was in terrible pain. He looked at his hands and, seeing how swollen and wounded they were, became worried. He was pulled from his worry with a question, asked by Somers, one of the shop owners in the village.

"Why ever have you stopped? You can't stop, you can't ever stop. Ever..."

And for once, Ash didn't know what to say.

"Evil, the whole village. All of it. Every last inch of it. It's Evil and it sickened the soil, rose into the sky, and drained into the waters and which infected all those miserable people. It was a curse, and it was nothing more than they deserved."

The old woman who called herself Hush had been the first thing Queen Messy had seen upon exiting her coach and she wasn't sure if she was thankful to the woman for being there. She had approached Messy with food and ale, which was welcome, though she was just as distressed at her infectious misery.

"But if such a place exists then why have I never heard of it? Why have I never heard of Umpton? And why would I not go there to see if I could aid them?"

The old woman laughed, and as she did ale spilled from between her cracked lips.

"Such as they can't *be* aided, lass. A young man went there just yesterday thinking he might save them and there he remains, trapped by his wish to help them. Trapped by the curse. Ah, but how can such a good soul as his refuse the wishes of a poor village that was abandoned by its Song Mother and thus cursed?"

"Song Mother, I've heard that name before, what was she?" Messy responded.

"HA! What indeed. She was a wicked thing that was no woman at all. She said she was a Song Mother of old but was far, far from it. She came from beyond the Thicket and lived amongst the people of your Kingdom as a child but as she grew she began calling others with her beautiful music and with it she spread misery and addiction wherever she went. She moved from village to village, going from these lands to the lands further out and then back beyond the Thicket from time to time to whatever lay there. She was a mother as much as I am - which is to say, dear, not one at all."

Messy didn't know what to say. She knew, at least a little, about the Song Mothers, who had been here before the Mistresses of Magic had appeared but this other was something new. She had heard tales from mother and from her advisors that there had been those in the Kingdom of Man who had sown deception and evil but it was thought that they had faded with the wars and the rise of the Mistresses. She could bring the sun back, could bring smiles to people but could she really face this? Could she cure the ills of a curse? Could she face something that might create that curse when she could barely face herself these days? Messy looked up into the sky and saw only clouds and again, far, far away, there was a dark shape that seemed to appear then disappear and just seeing it sent a shiver down her spine. How could it be that there was still so much darkness here when she had brought back the sun? She let out a long sigh.

"Then how can I help this place? I am the Queen, and have much power so what can I do to help heal them of this curse and affliction?"

The old woman laughed and spat out some of the black muck she had been chewing on.

"Ah, yer a Queen all right, not that I wondered with

that carriage and the scent and look of ya but, yeah, just like the others, like yer own mother Anamare. Yes, dear, you are indeed Queen, and as such are a Mistress of Magic but even magic cannot cure some things. Some ills have to be gone through, experienced. Some trials cannot be avoided. And dear, I can look in your eyes and see that you too are cursed, though ye may not see what it is yet. And if you ask me, some curses cannot be lifted unless with fire." The old woman smiled at Messy, her mouth full of false teeth made of some sort of gemstones that seemed to glow green. Messy felt sick. Being near the woman made her uneasy and it seemed as if she knew more, far more than she was letting on and it scared her. And it suddenly struck her - *How could she be so powerful and yet so helpless to aid these people? How was that possible?*

"I can see it in yer eyes that you doubt me, young miss and I tell you what I would tell me own daughter if I had one – see for yourself. But see with open eyes and an open heart and be willing to admit that some problems even a Mistress of Magic and Queen cannot solve. Be willing to see that some darkness can never be reached by the sun, no matter how bright it be."

"Yes, well, thank you ma'am. I, I uh, shall consider your words and choose my next actions carefully. There is much in this land I can do, much that I *must* do, but perhaps you are right and there are still some things I cannot do so I may not have time to aid that village but perhaps I can send my people to look in on them."

"Yes, yes lass, do that, you do just that. Now off with ya. 'Tis the Dark Lands and the Great Thicket you're after and those places are still a great ways away."

Messy's heart caught in her chest. She hadn't told this woman where she was headed, had she?

"But how would you know where I am going? I never told you that. Not once."

"Off with ya girl and here, take this blanket as a token from an old lady to the new Queen, take it and remember me."

The woman reached into a dark leather bag she had sitting beside the stone she sat upon and from that bag she handed the Queen a blanket. It took her a moment to realize what it was but as soon as Messy saw the blanket a shriek escaped her for the blanket was made from the skins of Meep Sheep and Bumble Kitties, a long, furry tail hanging at each corner as testament to that fact. Messy had never seen anything so horrible in all her life and her blood ran cold. Messy stood quickly, knocking the plate of food and ale from her knees and she dashed for the carriage, suddenly thankful she had passed on the stew the woman had offered as she returned to the safe darkness of her coach and set it in motion again. The old woman's laughter followed her for a mile as the carriage sped off, and it haunted many of her dreams thereafter. There had been something so familiar about the woman, so terribly familiar but she wasn't sure why.

For her part Lady Hush seemed disappointed that the Queen did not want the blanket she had made just the night before, on her way out to where the young woman was camped. She pushed the blanket back into its bag and grabbed the ladle and got herself some more stew, smiling that she had not wasted any of the meat from the blanket. In a moment the sun appeared and the woman frowned and cleared her throat. The old woman took a deep breath and began singing a most lovely song and all around her the grass died, and the tree that she was leaning upon slumped over to one side and its leaves fell off and far above her, thick, black clouds covered the sun. And seeing this, the woman smiled and finished her meal, her head full of flames.

All went to darkness for Ashley but the music

still played, his hands still moving, though his mind had fallen into the mists of unconsciousness. In that dimness Ashley dreamt, dreamt of a great long row of trees that huddled together and held a great blackness behind them, as if holding it back and standing guard before those trees was a withered old man that stood before a small, unimposing home. The man smiled at Ash as if expecting him and he pointed to the great woodland and frowned and nodded. Ash wasn't sure what he meant by that but before he could ask the man spoke to him.

"Son, sometimes we must leave behind the very thing we love most in order to move forward and find the essence of that love. True love exists whether or not that which we love exists - it exists on its own. You understand, Ashley? You gotta let it go. You gotta let it go and move on, there are greater things ahead..."

Ashley woke to silence and grayness and a symphony of pain. He looked at his hands and they were red hooks with the guitar cradled in them loosely. He opened his eyes wide and saw he was still in the Square of Umpton, the people of the village huddled nearby and sleeping around him. His kitty companions were nowhere to be seen but he had known they were not comfortable here, were not happy, and now he cursed himself from not trusting their instincts. He felt they were safe though, which was what mattered. Had the old woman been here he might be more concerned but she was long gone so now he must worry about himself. As much pain as he was in, Ash had enough of his senses to know that something seemed wrong and in an instant he saw it – someone had placed a bolt through the head of the guitar and had tied a string through that bolt and the string was tied to both Pan and Adle, who slept nearest, atop the edge of the fountain. Ash studied the guitar and it was stained red now, even the strings and there was no way he could unhook the guitar from the string and not wake the cousins. Ash looked around and saw everyone was still fast asleep, despite the gray dawn that was approaching.

Though everyone still looked young they were aging again, hour by hour and the village seemed to have been painted over night with gray that seemed to be waiting patiently to return. And looking at the people he got the same feeling he had about Pan and Adle, that they were not nearly as young as his music had made them but were wearing their youth as a mask. Ash felt sick and needed water but the first thing he needed to do was to get free, and to do that he had to get the guitar out of his hands.

Simple.

But it wasn't.

Ash closed his eyes against the pain and tried to open his hands but nothing happened. He tried

again and nothing. Again. Nothing. Ashley's heart started racing as the dark shadows began to retreat into light gray ones. He looked up and saw that some of the people were stirring in their sleep, not far from waking. Time was running out. Ash looked at his hands and cringed at how they looked and knew there was no way he could go through another day like he just had. There was no way. He took a breath and closed his eyes and concentrated, concentrated until there were stars in the darkness behind his eyes and slowly, slowly his hands opened up and his grip on the guitar loosened. Just as he was about to force them completely open though the guitar's weight shifted and it began to slide across his palms towards the cobblestone street. Panicked, Ash closed his hands quickly and winced with the pain. Ash opened his eyes and realized this was his last chance before people began waking up. He leaned forward so that the guitar was lying on the stone street and then focused everything he could on his hands and opened them both suddenly so that he was finally free again.
Free.

Ashley took a deep breath and noticed for the first time how the air smelled of sour milk, and, looking over at Pan and Able, how they didn't look young at all but looked as if they were wearing masks to make it appear they were young, like everyone else. And it wasn't just their eyes, but their hands, and their mouths that looked old to him. Ash's breath stopped short as he stood slowly up and saw that he had been right and that all of the people there looked the same as Pan and Able – as if though they wore the appearance of youth they were all in fact old, very old, and had been all along. Whatever curse had been laid on the town had been placed there years or even decades earlier and now they were all old, old but wanting to be young, wanting it bad enough to force him to make them young at any cost.

It had all been a lie, and Ashley had fallen for it. Perhaps they had lost their music, and perhaps they had all lost their joy but the land was dead because they had stopped tending it, and he saw that from the full wells he had passed on his way into village, and the rusty tools he saw everywhere he looked. The people here survived by sheering and selling the milk of Bloo Moos, the rare cows that were all but extinct in the Kingdom of Man due to people killing them for food, which was said to be a delicacy, and, for places like Umpton, were nothing more than a way to make money. Ash turned and started to run but before he made it out of the village square he heard the voice of Pan, weak and feeble, calling after him, begging him to stay but he ignored it and ran as fast and hard as he could, ran until his chest was on fire and he could run no more. Ash ran and ran and when Ash finally stopped and took his eyes off his feet and the ground, he found himself in a great

green field, under a bright yellow sun, and was not far from a river where he could clean up and get something to drink. He prayed he was far enough away from the town, that he was safe, but he knew that whether he was or not he could go no further. Ash started walking slowly towards the water and as he walked he looked down at his hands and his face flushed with shame at having left the guitar Kelvin had given him behind, and for having been fooled by the people of Umpton. He let out a sob and felt tears on his cheeks. Suddenly he was so exhausted and overcome with heartbreak that he fell to his knees and started to cry. The water was still so far away and he felt so weak and just as all hope seemed to be lost.
How could he hope to help anyone with real problems, with real need, or even face what lay ahead at the Thicket if he couldn't even help himself?

Ash was deep in though when from behind him there came a sudden and loud, "Mooooooooooooooo!" Ashley turned and saw that there was a Bloo Moo inflating itself and floating up into the sky, its blue tail swishing with anger as three bumble kitties hovered nearby. The kitties, seeing that Ash was watching, gave up their pursuit of the cow and slowly made their way towards their friend, whose tears had suddenly become laughter. The kitties finally got to Ash and then hovered around him, their paws batting playfully at him as he doubled up with laughter. The kitties dropped to the ground and rubbed against Ashley and he got up, still sore but feeling lighter now and he began walking slowly towards the water and away from the darkness of Umpton, and as he and his friends went, they took up a song and at that moment nothing in the world, not even the angry Bloo Moo, was lighter than Ash was at that moment.

It had been a good day for No One, who had gotten his first restful sleep in weeks during an afternoon nap, and the clouds in his heart had parted, at least for the moment. Truth be told, the last year had not been kind to the old man, who, once the new Queen had taken up her position, had known that the Time of Change was nearing. The Thicket had been restless the day Anamare had relinquished her office and they had not quieted for more than a week at a time since. No One had been watching closely to see what the Thicket would do, if something might emerge, but nothing had, at least as far as he had seen. It was rare that things left the Thicket but it *had* happened once before, the day young Queen Lizabelle, the third Queen of the Kingdom of Man, had fallen from a horse and had been gravely injured. A deep sadness had struck the Kingdom and it was feared that, should she fall, the restless Tribe of the Valley would encroach into the land. No One had done something that was forbidden, something he had never told any of the travelers that visited him over the years, he had used a secret doorway that stood hidden behind a deep patch of brush and beneath a great root. No One took only his cloak and walking stick into the Great Thicket, hoping that would be all he might need as he didn't intend to stay long. There was an odor about the place that was like freshly baked bread but, too, there was a scent of decay, and of rotting leaves. No One was quick in doing what he must, not wanting to spend too much time in the forbidden land for he had heard the same stories everyone else in the Kingdom had, and far, far worse. No One went into the Thicket far enough to enter a clearing but beyond that place lay the old place with thousands of trees that glittered and glowed and which called his eyes to them and wouldn't release him. Suddenly he forgot his duty, his purpose, and stood transfixed by the trees, wanting only to walk back to them and to hear their songs. Then a voice, a whisper came and surrounded him as someone spoke –

You do not belong here, No One of Man. Your purpose is honorable though so you may take what you must and be gone. Look around you, many of your kind have fallen doing just as you do now, looking at the trees, and I warn you that there are far worse things here than trees. Far worse. Now do what you must and be gone.

There was a laugh in the whisper, unspoken but there, and as No One came to his senses he looked down and saw that all around him were hundreds of bones, human bones, and amidst all of them was the seed that he needed, the blue seed from one of the old trees that he had come here for and must leave with. He quickly snatched up the seed and ran back the way he had come as quickly as he could and from behind him there was a great clamor, though he dared not look to see what it was. He had since learned much from the Thicket, and from the voice that had saved him that day, but at that moment, he was a very little man in a very big, very dangerous forest, but he made it out of there, and made it out with his prize.

His father had told him, a great many years earlier, of a breed of cow that used to roam the wilds of the Kingdom of Man, a cow whose milk was, like the cow itself, blue, and which had healing properties. The cows had been hunted into near extinction though and had rarely been seen again. Something told No One that this seed, if planted, and loved, and if bathed in milk and honey, might bring one of those cows here to help the young Queen. That night he planted the seed and poured a mixture of milk and honey atop the soil and he went to sleep. The next morning he awoke to a great deal of noise and he found two great blue cows eating flowers from his flower garden. Not thinking, the man ran at the cows to shoo them away but as soon as he neared them they inflated suddenly with air and started floating up and away from him. It was the strangest thing he had ever seen and perplexed him deeply. He knew he needed that milk though so he began working on a plan, and, late that evening, after dozens upon dozens of attempts, he was able to lull one of the cows into sleep so he could milk it.

As soon as that was done the cow let out an angry 'moo' and inflated and the two floated off into the night. It mattered little though for he had the milk, which he sent on to the Queen in the hopes it might save her. The night he learned that the Queen was well came when he received the only visit he had ever had out at the Thicket from any of the Queens. She came alone and stayed long enough to kiss him on his cheeks, and to thank him for saving her. Then she was gone. It was a day he had never forgotten over his many, many years, and it was one which he still held close at hand whenever his heart turned dark.

It had been many years since that day he had come out of the Thicket with his prize and in all that time nothing else had come out, though many people and *things* had gone in but so far he had never seen anything come out, though he knew that the things in the Thicket wanted nothing more than to be freed onto the lands. And just as he knew that, he knew too that there were things that kept those things at bay, kept them in check, but if the Thicket should fall whatever darkness that lay within would be released, and it was a darkness that no sunlight could chase away. He had kept the Kingdom *and* the Thicket safe for a great many years but he knew trouble was coming, and it was a deep trouble. He wished there was something he might do to stop it but there was nothing to be done until Ashley and the Queen joined him. So, unable to do anything but wait, No One went about tending his garden and cleaned the area around his home to keep his mind occupied. Just as he began whistling an old song from his childhood he caught the scent of something burning and looked up and saw that on the horizon there was smoke coming from a great fire, and around that fire he saw dots, hundreds and hundreds of black dots, black dots which were people.

They were coming.

After all these years of peace, the people of the Kingdom of Man were coming for the Thicket, and it seemed they meant to burn it down. It may not be that night, or the next, but the day was coming fast, and No One knew it. And as soon as the Thicket was down, the darkness would within it would envelope the world.

Time was running out.

It would be kind to say that Queen Messy had finally found some peace and rest as No One had but it would be a lie. The truth is that Miss Messy found no peace and no rest as she ran from the company of the old woman of Umpton. Messy pushed the carriage as fast and hard as it would go in the hope of distancing herself, not knowing that she may have saved Ashley from his fate and perhaps the village from its spell had she gone there but, it was as Lady Hush said, there were some things even the Queen couldn't do, and just then, she had other, bigger things to worry about. Messy, blinded with fear, went past everything known in the Kingdom of Man and when she finally stopped the carriage, a full day after her journey had begun; she was in the Barren Fields, the place that bordered the Unclaimed Waste which was said to be haunted after the long years of war. She was on the outer edge of her Kingdom and as near to a different kingdom as she had ever come. The Plains King ruled the place beyond the Fields and over the hills and it was said that he, above all others, hated the Kingdom of Man the most, it being said that his great grandfather had been spurned by a Mistress of Magic and thus declaring war so many years earlier. Messy had no idea how close to danger she was though as she was overcome with an exhaustion that was almost painful the Queen stopped the carriage in a grove of trees, locked everything down tight, and slipped under her covers and fell deep into dreams.

As she had for weeks before, she found herself in the Mother Wood, the forest of the Queens. Messy woke into the dream standing in a small area where the sun had broken through in the dark woods, her bare feet deep in the grass and weeds and her nightgown soaked in the sweat from the previous day. Messy shook her head to clear it, understanding she was in a dream but wanting to be aware for it, conscious for it, and ready for it. The woods were silent but she could feel eyes watching her and knew she wasn't alone.

*But what if you **are** alone, Mistress?*

The voice came from the trees but she wasn't sure where. She took a step forward and to the edge of the light she stood in.

Wouldn't do that, m'lady. Not at all. Not safe in the darkness. No, not at all girl.
Messy stood on the edge of darkness and squinted her eyes to see if she could see who had spoken and saw no one.

Oh yes, No One is here, but deeper in, child, far deeper in. Here you are alone. All alone. Well, except for me, that is.

Messy's heart was racing and she stood on her tiptoes and looked into the darkness and saw nothing but trees. The trees, which were thick and tall but were like all the other trees she had seen her whole life but, beyond them, far deeper into the wood, where it was completely dark, there were trees that glittered, trees that sparkled, and she wished to be there.

In time, dear, in time. But not yet. No. Not yet. For now, what do you see?

Messy dropped back flat onto her feet and looked around her and saw trees, trees, and more trees. There was nothing else to see. Nothing but…wait, wait, there *was* something else to see. Sitting in the trees, in the limbs were Bumble Kitties which were deep in sleep, and as she looked, she saw that the trees were thick with them. There too, off to her left, bounding from shadow to shadow was an Iperbah, which was a breed of animal that was said to be the shyest of all the animals of the Kingdom yet was there, back in the trees. Messy heard a mooing and turned around and saw a Bloo Moo grazing on the opposite side of her circle but as soon as she moved it saw her and inflated itself and floated up and out of sight. Messy laughed, the first time she had done that in days. She was still laughing when she heard it, heard the familiar sound she had not heard in so long that her heart had all but lost hope of hearing it again. Yet there it was. Small, but there.

'Meep'.

Messy's mouth broke into a wide grin and she heard it again, closer, and then again, coming her way. She couldn't see it but she could feel it, as she had always felt the sheep when they were near, as her hands went warm and her fingers tingled as they had when she had created them the first time. And there, there it was, fluffy and white and coming out of the darkness to her, its blue eyes almost shining, and as soon as she saw it she ran towards it, leaving the circle and entering the darkness of the woods. As soon as she crossed the threshold she was struck by how warm the air was, and how hard the ground was and how dark the dark was. It took her a moment to realize she was out of the sunlight, where the air had been far cooler, and the ground far softer, but none of that mattered, all that mattered was that she see her friend, her lost little…

'Kreeeeeeeep'.

The voice seemed to echo through the woods and sent a chill down Messy's back just as it turned the gentle hum in her hands to a terrible tremor. Messy stopped running and as she stopped she heard the ground beneath her crunch and she looked down and beneath her were hundreds and hundreds of bones that stretched out into the darkness and made up the fabric of the ground. Her skin ran cold. This wasn't the Mother Wood at all. This was, this was… the Thicket.

'*Kreeeeeeeep*'.

Messy looked up and saw it, the thing she had seen before in her dream, the thing the other her called a Kreep Sheep, its red eyes glowing in the darkness, its gray fur mottled and matted and its horns yellow from age. It flew at her slowly and gracelessly and was nothing like a Meep Sheep. Messy opened her mouth to scream but nothing came out so she turned to run but couldn't, her feet too deep in the bones to move. She looked up and the Bumble Kitties watched with red eyes, their forked tongues hanging out, and the Bloo Moo was now blood red as it hovered nearby. Everything she saw watched her with hungry eyes and she couldn't escape. She spun her head around and still the Kreep Sheep came. And if it touched her what then? What then?

Come now dear, is it so terrifying, to look darkness in the eyes?

Messy closed her eyes and bit her lip, pleading with herself to wake up, begging herself to open her eyes.

What if you are already awake?

Tears stung Messy's eyes and she raised her hands to

protect herself but suddenly she was awake and in the bed in the carriage and was safe again though the voice still spoke, echoing in her head as she brushed the sleep from her eyes.

What if you embraced the darkness? What if you let it come? What if you became Queen of another place, another land? What if you let the darkness come and flood the world? Would it all be so bad? Would it be so bad if the pain went away? Would it?

Messy pinched herself but felt nothing and the Kreep Sheep dropped to the ground and approached her. The voice, like that of an old woman was familiar. It seemed so close. Just as she was about to figure out who was calling to her though there was another voice. A voice like a light, like a beacon.

Messy, Mistress Messy, do you believe everything you hear? Everything you see? What if this is all just a dream and all you have to do is to wake up? What if the light you are looking for is in yourself? What if you just... ***woke up?***

Messy awoke and pulled the bedding back but saw nothing on her legs or feet to make her feel as if she had really been gone but there was a sick feeling deep in her stomach and she knew that somehow she had been in those woods surrounded by darkness. Messy sat up in bed and brought her legs up to her chest and stared at the closed shades and the dim sun that slipped through them, wondering when the nightmares would end and whether she was strong enough to end them herself.

For Ashley, the reality of what he had been through was finally setting in, and the weight of it was great upon him. He had stayed the entire and night by the side of the water as his friends purred and rubbed on him. The pain in his hands was something like he had never experienced before and he was still unable to open them completely so he wrapped them as best he could in Lily Reed and let them rest. It was hard, too, to deal with the way he had been used by the people of Umpton. He had honestly thought he had helped them, had felt as if he had done some good but it had all been a lie. A lie. That bitterness was hard to accept, those dark clouds and hidden stars so hard to take for one so used to living in the sunlight and shade but it was something he had no choice but to live with, and to learn from. And that was the hardest part – learning from it. But, as he sat on the grass with his feet and hands dipped in the cool waters, and his friends chasing Butterbugs and Squiddlepops nearby, he remembered another time, not as long ago as it seemed, he faced another challenge, and had learned from it otherwise he wouldn't be where he was today.

A boy named Glen had come to his village with a

song like Ashley had, but which drew more people than Ash ever had, and it had broken Ash's heart to admit that, but, in admitting it, he released himself from his need to perform in his home village and to people in general. He released himself from the need to feel loved and adored for his music, and in so doing, got closer to the music itself. He remembered that it was the music he loved, the music he had been taught to love by a friend gone but not forgotten, and it was that love, that pure love of music which he clung to now, when things seemed darkest. He had seen how your passion and the love of the thing you held most dear could turn ugly, and how people could drain you of that passion and take it from you. He had almost let it happen before, and had let it happen this time, and it hurt, but beneath that hurt, there was a song. Ashley Pickles smiled to himself and kicked his feet in the water as some fish swam near, and Ash reached over his back for his guitar and felt nothing.

The smile fell away.

His guitar. The one his lost friend Kelvin had given him.

It was gone.

Ashley spun around and saw only the green grass behind him and the long trail he'd come down and nothing more. Again Ash's heart sank and his head fell into his hands and there was nothing to do to stop these tears at the loss of something so precious to him. His hands, which ached so much, may never

even be able to play a guitar again but just the same the loss was like losing his friend all over again. Ash went cold all over and forgot everything – why he was there, what he was doing, where he was going and what it was he loved. Just as the clouds were covering his heart completely though there came a shadow over the sun, a shadow that descended and covered Ash completely. The Bumble Kitties looked up, saw what it was, and gave up their pursuit of bugs and bounded for Ash.
They were too late.
The shadow landed beside Ash and looked at him for a moment before speaking.

"Meep."

Ashley seemed not to have heard it.

"Meep!"

Again, nothing. So, one last time it spoke.

"*Meep!*"

This time Ashley did hear it and when he looked up he had two big blue eyes staring at him from inches away. Ash pulled his head back and the creature moved closer, hovering on wings that looked like those of a bumble bee and which were attached to a small, fluffy sheep's body. Ash had heard of these but had never seen one up close. Its eyes radiated light blue and were almost hypnotizing and looking into them Ashley felt only peace and calm. Ash wasn't sure what to do but as he sat there in a stupor the Meep Sheep leaned forward and butted its head against his own softly then fluttered around so it plopped down beside him and then it butted its head against him again, this time into his arm. Ash shook his head, unsure what to do and it butted against him again then nudged his arm twice. Ashley tilted his head to the side, the tears drying on his face, and lifted his arm, and as soon as he did the Meep Sheep wiggled its way under it and against his side, and, almost by reflex Ash brought his arm back down and squeezed the sheep. As soon as he did he was filled with sudden warmth, as if the clouds in him had parted and the sun was back in full and without even knowing it, he smiled. The sheep looked up at him and let out another 'meep' before wiggling its way out from under his arm. Ash patted its fluffy head and no sooner had he done it than it took wing and was up and gone again into the clouds.

Just like that.

Ash laughed and watched his kitty friends fly up into the sky to try to follow the sheep but they either couldn't fly as high as it did or simply lost interest so they came back down and buzzed around his head and batted at him with their paws for a moment and then dropped down to the tree beside the water for another nap. Ash stood up and stretched as he thought over what was to come next. He would find something to eat, get a good night's rest, and then he had work to do. A lot of work to do. He could look to the horizon and see the Great Thicket. It was a day's journey but if he got going in the morning, and really moved, he could be there by nightfall. There were clouds at the horizon, and beyond them, beyond the Thicket, what was there?

He smiled.

He smiled because whatever happened, whatever lay ahead, he had three friends who had been with him through everything and remained, he had his music, and more importantly, he had himself. Whatever else was taken from him - he had that. Whatever tomorrow held he still had that.

The first drops of a warm Spring rain began to fall and Ash began to sing.

Along the Thicket there was movement, noise, anger. It sensed that people were gathering, people with fire, and while it had happened before, long before, this time seemed grimmer than ever. Had No One not eyes to see it, he could have just taken the signs of the Thicket to know how bad things were. Queen Lizzabelle had warned him this day would come, and he had never doubted it but, as with all fear of the inevitable, he had hoped it would never really happen. As No One stood on his hill, Sighing

Pipe in hand and watched as the fires in the distance drew nearer, as the numbers of people grew along the borderlands to the West. No One blew his pipe and the anger in the Thicket calmed but he knew it would return. He could do many things, and had done them over the course of his watch, but to stop this tide, he would need help. He could fight if he had to, could try to speak sense to the people, but in the end they would do as they wished if he was alone. His only hope was that help would arrive in time.

Messy paced beside her carriage as she had for much of the late day and now as night fell. She had slept while she could during the day but there was no peace for her there. She had looked into her mirror earlier as she was washing up and was horrified to see that the rainbow colors of her hair had faded to dull grays and black and that she looked pale and old from everything going on. Worse though was that she wasn't the only thing that had changed.
Outside things were no better.
The Carriage itself was covered with a thick layer of dust and mud from her travels and all around her was brown and gray. No grass grew in this part of the Kingdom, the trees were gray and hunched to the side, and even the air left a bitter taste in her mouth. Adding everything up, she knew where she

was and cursed herself for being here. This was a dead place, a haunted place, and the only time people or creatures in the land came here was to die. She had read many books about the place as a child, fascinated by the horrors that were rumored to have been done here, and the specters that lurked here but, now that she saw it all for herself, all she felt was sad. Off in the distance she could see the deep gouges that had been made into the ground during the war and along the far hills she saw the remnants of one of the forts where the people of her Kingdom had held the incoming raiders back. This was the place the tides of war had turned, but so many had died because of that turn. Had a brave knight not managed to stop the Black Fire before it was unleashed all may have been lost. Messy looked sadly past the hills and mourned that to this day her people and the people of that land were distant to one another. She took her eyes off of her surroundings and looked off to the east of the neighboring kingdom and saw the tops of the trees that made up the Great Thicket not even a day's journey away. She should have been there by now but she had been meandering and letting herself get distracted under the guise of wanting to see her lands. At first it had been the Queen's business she was on, visiting villages and finding out what she could do to make life better for the people but along the way she had lost her way. She lost her way when she realized how big the job ahead of her was and that Meep Sheep alone would not make the people happy, nor would any of her 'little tricks' as one man had called her magics. It would take hard work, and years untold to heal the wounds along the lands and it scared her because she had no idea how to start, and where to go.

How had her mother done it all those years?

Her mother had taken trips around the land, yes, and had seen many people, but she had always had a song for her daughter, or a story, or even just time to spare. How had she done it?

The answer eluded Messy so she returned to pacing back and forth. She had seen much in that moment of looking at the Thicket for along with the clouds, and the trees, she had seen the thick black smoke of fire. She had seen the growing fear in the Kingdom personified by what had to be a traveling mob, as with the fire came distant voices She knew things were not good but had they gotten so bad, so quickly? Then she thought of the nightmares she had been having, of the thing that seemed to be ever lurking just out of sight, and wondered if such darkness was playing itself out all across the Kingdom, pushing its own agenda forward. She had never suspected something so awful could be happening. .

But hadn't she?

She remembered being in the village of Quar and how happy they were to see her, happy at least on the surface but beneath their smiles there was something else, there was anger. And why were they angry? Because they feared her, and she knew it. They feared that she had a power that none of the other Queens had. Yes, they could bring the sunshine, and yes, they, like the Song Mother's of old, could weave wonders with music but none of them could create things the way Messy could. None of them could form things out of clay and have them become reality, something Messy had been in love with at first but which, as time passed, she had come to hate. After making many Meep Sheep she had suddenly, and secretly, stopped. Stopping because of a dark question that formed in her mind one night – *what if she made something dangerous?*
And she didn't have an answer.
So she paced.
And as she paced, darkness fell.

As Messy paced the Ghost Worms started their nightly migrations and the ground took on an eerie red glow, though she didn't notice, being lost in thoughts of her mother. If only her mother were here, she would know what to do. Anamare had been one of the most renowned of the Queens and during her reign the seeds of peace had finally begun

to flourish but there was fear in the people now, as Messy and her Counselors knew well and if she didn't truly convince the people she could rule then all the work her mother and the other Queens had done would be for nothing.
Yes, she *had* to convince them.

From the sky a shadow descended slowly, so slowly.

Yes, she had to convince them. But who were *they* to need convincing? She was the Queen, not them? She was the Mistress of Magic, not them. How dare they question her rule? How dare they believe they knew better than she did?

The shadow came closer and as it came, the Ghost Worms burrowed back into the ground and left darkness in their wake.

She was fine. She was doing a good job and, and if they didn't see it then who cared? Maybe they deserved war. Maybe they deserved the worst. Maybe it was time for the sun to finally go away for good and for the darkness to reign. Maybe it was time to leave them to the darkness. Messy sneered as she kicked the dirt.

And from behind and above her the shadow settled over Messy and uttered a single sound - "*Kreep.*"

Messy looked up in horror and saw a dark shape that was black against a gray sky and her heart screamed. It couldn't be. She could hear the whisper of the thing's wings, a sound like dry leaves rustling in the wind, and as she watched it the thing dropped to the ground. Its eyes were twin fires that sat between two dark shadows that erupted crookedly from its head. It was the same size and shape as a Meep Sheep but this was something else, something made of mud, not clay, of shadow, not light. It took a step towards Messy and let out another '*Kreeeeeeeep*' and took a step. Messy looked around and saw nothing to protect herself with then caught sight of the Carriage and headed for it. Just as she was within feet of the Carriage though the shadow dropped down in front of her, blocking her path. Messy looked around again and saw nothing and nowhere to go. The Kreep Sheep stepped towards her and lowered its head and spoke again – *Kreep*. It hopped forward, fluttering its wings briefly to gain the air then coming down less than five feet from her. The woods. Messy looked past the Kreep Sheep and there were woods, or rather a collection of dead trees that, in any other situation, she would never think to enter but now she had no choice, she had to get away. She had to get away or die.

Die.

Messy turned to run but her legs gave out and she fell face forward onto the hard ground, her head connecting and filling the world with stars. So this was how it was going to end for her, for the last Queen, the last Mistress? This was how she ended her days, running away, or lying in the dirt, not standing and facing her fate. Oh, but the darkness, the darkness that called to her seemed so safe, so comforting and so...cold. So dead. The tears that had been coming for what seemed like months and which never seemed to have stopped for her finally stopped and it was suddenly replaced by anger. Messy remembered a day spent with her mother when she was still just a girl, and everything suddenly came clear.

She had been playing out in the courtyard with a friend and had gone inside for some water where she found her mother Anamare sitting in the kitchen with her head in her hands. At first Messy thought her mother was laughing, the way her hunched shoulders were shaking, but as she moved closer she saw that she wasn't laughing at all but was crying, something she had never seen her mother do. Messy froze for a moment, unsure what to do but, seeing her mother that way moved something in her and in turn she found herself walking across the tile. Her mother must not have realized she was there because she kept crying, though silently, and without thinking Messy put her hand on her mother's shoulder and her mother turned, startled. Seeing who it was, she wiped the tears away and patted Messy's hand.

"I am sorry, my dear. A daughter shouldn't have to see her mother cry."

"But you see me cry, you see me cry and you make me feel better. Can, can I make you feel better, mom?"

Anamare leaned forward and kissed Messy's head below her rainbow locks and took her daughter by the shoulders.

"Messy, there is something you need to know, something I wanted to tell you when you were older and closer to being Queen yourself but I see now that this is the perfect time. Messy, you will never do anything in your life harder and more heartbreaking than to lead the people of this Kingdom, but with that, you may never do anything more rewarding or important. You are the only thing in my life that is more important to me than this beautiful Kingdom, but that is not to say it will ever be easy. Today is one of the hard days, one of the very hard days, but it is only one day and tomorrow is another day, and it may be better, or it may be worse, but honey, it is a new day and with your love, with the love of the people who believe in me, I know everything will be OK. Sometimes you must face the very darkness you fear to find the light in yourself and in others. Do you understand what I am saying, honey? Does this make sense?"

And Messy stood there in front of her mother, blushing with shame because she didn't understand, she didn't understand at all and doubt filled her like lead. Her mother, seeming to sense all this, leaned forward and kissed her forehead

"There is no shame in not understanding, Messy, just as there is no shame in not knowing what to do. What you must always remember, no matter what happens, is that as long as you have yourself, as long as you have that belief in yourself then you have hope. Hope is the key. It's only when you give up on yourself that you finally lose all hope and all color falls out of the world and becomes darkness. Now go play, my sweet little bee, and let me get back to making this a Kingdom we can be proud of again."

Messy found out later that this had been during the peace talks with the last of the Kingdoms that had been distressing her mother so much with talk of a new war, and when Messy had found her mother it had been when it looked as if the talks would fall through. And if the talks fell through the war might be renewed, something Anamare vowed to not let happen. After speaking with her daughter Anamare went back into the negotiations and got the peace treaty she wanted. There had peace since.
Peace until now.
Since Anamare had left the Kingdom to be with the

other Mistresses of Magic in the Mother Wood there had been a deep seated doubt in whether Messy was up to the job the other Queens had done and within that doubt were the seeds of unrest, seeds that, if left to grow, might bring the Kingdom to war once more. Messy had tried, with the gifts of her magic, and by bringing the sunshine back, and even by bringing the Carnival King through the Kingdom from time to time but nothing she had done had convinced the people she could rule them and keep them safe. It was time to make them believe.
She had been a Mistress of Magic but never a Queen.
It was time to be the Queen.

Messy rolled over so she was on her back and pushed her arms beneath her and stood up, slowly and painfully, and faced the Kreep Sheep. It stood ten feet from her, its head low and its red eyes glowing in the shadows as it watched her. *She* was in the woods, the woman that had been in her dreams, haunting her, and if she went in, she may not return. She may run, she may fall, or she may just let loose the darkness in the Thicket herself, things she might have done before, but not now. Not anymore. So she stood and faced the Kreep Sheep. The two of them stood and watched one another for a few moments before Messy took a step towards it. It stood its ground and she took another step, then another, and another, and another until she was directly in front of it and could reach out and touch it if she wished. It looked up at her, silent and watchful.

"I feel as if you have been stalking me for years, little Kreep Sheep. I feel as if I dreamed of your nightmares the night after I created your brethren, the Meep Sheep. I have been running from you for all these weeks for fear of what you might do. For fear that you might kill me, or worse, someone else. I always feared you were there, hiding just out of sight, hiding beneath everything I made, just waiting to be freed. All this time though I have been running not from you but from myself and my power. Whatever you are, my friend, you are as alone as I am now, and if I can offer you anything, I can offer you friendship, and what you do with it is for you to decide."

Having spoken, Messy knelt down and opened her arms wide to the Kreep Sheep and smiled, the color, unknown to her, flooding back into her skin and hair. The Kreep Sheep stood watching her a moment then took a tentative step forward, then another, then another until it was within her grasp and as soon as it was she closed her arms around it in an embrace. Messy was shocked at how cold the Kreep Sheep was but in a moment her own warmth seemed to fill it and it warmed within her embrace. She squeezed it then and it replied with '*Kreeeeeeep*'. And Messy smiled. Whatever was going to happen

was going to happen but as Queen she had to love every creature of her Kingdom, whatever it was. As she hugged the Kreep Sheep something changed though.
Its course, wiry fur became soft, its horns disappeared, the red ran from its eyes and was replaced with a light blue and suddenly it proclaimed '*Meep! Meep!*'
Messy pulled away from the animal and saw she was embracing a Meep Sheep, and as she saw this she saw that the ground was coming back to life – the worms were reemerging, the color was coming back to the grass and as she watched buds sprouted in the trees, and slowly, so slowly, the wounds in the ground began to heal. Messy released the sheep and it pranced away, jumping up into the air and doing a spin before dropping back down to gallop back towards her, making her laugh as she hadn't laughed in weeks.

"Has it been you all along? Was it you that was following me? Was it you I was afraid of all this time?"

"Meep!"

From the woods there came the voice of an old man, though she could see no one there.

"Dear Queen, it was *you* that you were running

from, it was you all this time, though the old woman surely was there behind much of it, preying on your insecurity. But this was how it was meant to be, even if it was not how you wished it to be. You stopped running when you were ready to face your fears, and as soon as you faced your fear of failing as Queen you became the Queen. Everyone falters, but it is only when you give up on yourself that you truly fail. The woman, a wicked thing from days of old, could only hurt you as much as you let her and when you stopped running her power over you was gone. Now if only we can break that power she has over the rest of the Kingdom. I ask you, Queen Messy, are you ready to free your people and lead them?"

Messy did not ask to whom the voice belonged because she knew it was not the woman and that it meant her no harm. It was the second voice from the woods, the one that had lead her from the darkness. It didn't matter whose voice it was, what mattered was the question and her answer.

"I am."

"Then Queen, you know where you belong."

Messy turned and looked at her Carriage but knew that for this last part of the journey she must go by foot, so she did just that, and began walking towards the Great Thicket, and all around her the dead ground was giving birth to a new beginning.

War had come to the Great Thicket. After decades of peace the storms of war which had been held back by the sun of the Mistresses of Magic for so many years looked to finally be coming to a head. No One had been watching the storm grow, day by day, hour by hour and now it was at a head as thousands of people, none of them having slept more than a few scant hours in weeks, lined the countryside just down the hill from the Great Thicket. He had known this day would come, the Thicket had been the birthplace of rumor and fable and some things that were truly from nightmares and when things get bad you tend to turn to the closest boogeyman to blame and for the Kingdom of Man that was the Thicket. And No One could run to these people and beg them to reconsider, beg them to stop but the fire spoke louder now, as did the fear, and fear and anger tended to win out in these circumstances. Lady Hush, wanting to destroy the Thicket for so many decades, wanting only to spread darkness, and now was her chance. She had tried before, and when that had failed she had spread darkness person by person, town by town, always sowing the seeds of unhappiness and always there.

And now, now was her chance to truly do as she had always wanted, and that was to bring the reign of the Mistresses to an end and to set loose the Thicket. No One could fight her, fight them, and indeed he may have to should they come up the hill but for now he played his Sighing Pipe and waited.
They would come.
He knew they would come.
So he waited.
But as he waited, the fire along the plains grew.

Messy was the first to reach the plains that stood before the Great Thicket and it was worse than she had feared – there was a great mass of people that had gathered here and at the center of them was a bonfire that lit everything with an eerie red glow and tending it was a hunched woman she knew even from a distance. Messy strayed from the path that she had followed and entered the woods and brush that bordered the area so she could move without being seen. As she had traveled the path the Meep Sheep had followed her silently but now that she had moved to the woods it stopped short, uttered a small 'Meep' and rose into the air and moved up towards the small cottage on the hill and the man that stood beside it. Messy made her way through the woods and caught snatches of conversation from the people in the mob and it frightened her because it was talk of war and blood and hate and her name came up as much as the Thicket's and she knew that there would be no talking them out of this. They were under a dark spell and words alone would not calm them. At least not here, not now. She had to take the hill and see what the Thicket was, and who the person was that guarded it, this No One she had heard of but never met. Once she had seen these things she would see what was to be done. But to confront them now would be to incite them, to enrage them, and to light the fires on the Thicket herself. *Patience*, the voice of her mother cautioned, *patience my dear one and keep the faith in yourself. Then let come what may.* So she walked quietly through the brush and in no time she was cresting the hill and as she did she left the brush and looked on a man she had always known but never met.

Ashley and his companions came along a different path but came to the plains as Messy had, with a mix of fear and wonder in his heart. To see the people jumbled and massed together as the dawn of a new day came it was hard to look upon it all in awe and not imagine the greatness that could be achieved if all these people worked together on something good. All he could do now was tremble with fear at the destruction this many people could do should their minds be so inclined. Ashley Pickles could tell from the sight of the fires though that there was nothing good in the minds of these people and indeed, nothing in them at all but the fire itself. Something had to be done though, and maybe he was the one. Maybe he could reason with them. Maybe he could help them see how wrong they were. Whatever happened, he had to try. Ashley broke from the path and made his way towards the crowd and as soon as he did his companions darted for the sky and were not lazy then as they headed quickly towards the hill ahead where two figures were already gathered. Ashley headed for the first person he saw, a young boy not much younger than himself.

"What is all this, then? A celebration?" Being coy in his question but wanting as much of the truth as he might be able to get.

"Of a sort. We are here to burn the evil from this land, friend. The great woman who tends the fire called all of us here to overthrow the wicked Queen and the ills her kind have done here. We are here to burn down the Thicket for once and for all and to rid the land of its mischief."

"And what sort of mischief might a woodland get up to, friend?" Ash asked.

"Evil. Evil and nothing but evil. Why, we saw a dark thing flying for it not long ago, something with horns and evil red eyes that looked like a nightmare's version of a Meep Sheep. One of the men ahead there shot an arrow at it and took it to the ground and the witch up there on the hill gathered it up and carried it back to the house. The man that lives there is a wizard of old, descended from the Old Kings and it is said he controls the things that live in the woods."

Ashley had to force himself to speak as his heart raced beyond words alone with the realization that they'd killed a Meep Sheep.

"And, and what do they say *lives* in those woods?"

"Monsters. The old things that lurked the land and gobbled up women and children before even the Pandas roamed free. It was the monsters that brought the Old Kings to power, and which lead to the wars, which lead to the witches taking power, and which has lead to the misery and poverty we all suffer from, friend."

"The Queens were not witches though, friend. What of the good they did? What of the good that has happened in the Kingdom? What of the music and art and, and there have been no wars in ages, what of those things friend."

"Tricks, one and all. Tricks to make us believe we are safe, but we are not safe. We are never safe. Not so long as the Great Thicket stands and the witches rule. Until those things are gone we will never be happy. Never. *Never.*"

Ashley wandered away from the boy dazed, the depth of madness at hand finally clear to him. This was not a mindless mob, as he had hoped, no, it was an organic thing, a beast with many heads and a thirst for blood and fire, and all of it lead by a monstrous person who was pushing these people forward and fanning the flames of their fear. To call Queen Messy a witch and the old man on the hill a wizard, and, and to shoot down and kill a creature of the wilds, it was all too much and his hands and heart ached at all of it. How could things get so out of hand? He stumbled forward through the people, oblivious to what they said or did, whether they shoved him or touched him compassionately, it was all the same to him. Ashley was in another place as he made his way through the people and came close enough to the fire for it to singe his long brown hair and to hear the mad screams of the old woman. When that happened he was suddenly aware of everything, the sight, the sound, the feel of the crowd, and more than anything he was aware of the man that stood before him with pure rage in his eyes.

"WIZARD! Here he is, the wizard that killed my brother, here he is, friends, here is the first to taste the kisses of the fire today, the first and not the last by far!"
It was friend Pan, and beside him was friend Adle, both alive and well, though aged again, older than ever but wild and vibrant in their eyes. Their gnarled hands erupted from their robes and grabbed hold of Ashley and started pulling him toward the fire. Ash screamed and twisted in their grip but they were stronger than they looked.

"No, NO! Stop this, stop doing this before it is too late! I never harmed either of you, *any* of you. This is *wrong! Stop!*"

In answer to his pleas came laughter as more arms grabbed him and lifted him aloft and moved swiftly to the fire. The old woman screamed and waved them on toward the fire. There was nothing he could do. Nothing. Nothing until…and suddenly out of his mouth came a song. He hadn't even meant to sing, had meant in fact to scream but instead a song had come, a song that Kelvin had sung to him when they had first met, a song of loss and sadness and grief, a song written by a widow who had lost her husband and son to the wars of old. And as soon as he started singing the people around him stopped moving, and then the people around them stopped screaming, and then the people around *them* stopped pushing and all of a sudden all was still, all was calm and everyone stood motionless as they listened. Only the old woman screamed on, but no one listened to her now, their minds caught in the web of the song. Ashley sang on, his throat burning from the heat of the roaring fire but he sang on, knowing that if he faltered that he was doomed, the fire so close now, too close. As he sang the hands loosened their grips and he was slowly lowered until his feet were on the ground again and he looked and Able and Pan were both young again, young and crying, huddled together in shame. And were they all shamed? Yes, yes, shamed by the beauty of a song many had heard their own mothers sing when they were but children who had lost their own family members to the wars of old. Ashley didn't have much left to the song and was unsure if singing it again would hold them off long enough for him to make a break for the hill but he didn't need to worry as, at the sound of his singing, his three friends had come back for him and, when he looked up, he saw them hovering just above him. As he sang the last of the song, pouring the words over the crowd with as much emotion as he could in the hopes of reaching the part of them that might still be reasoned with, he reached up and grabbed the legs of two of the Bumble Kitties and they lifted him up and over the heads of the people and started flying towards the hill. They were well away from the fire as his song ended and it took only a moment for that rage in them to rekindle and the

voice of the old woman to take hold again as they realized they had been tricked. He heard one of the cousin's, either Able or Pan, he wasn't sure which, call him a wizard again and he was thankful for his friends then, who had saved him and who had him up high enough so that the reaching hands of the mob could not reach him. The rocks they threw reached him though, and they stung as they bounced off his prone body but he was glad for their hits as it meant he was alive, still alive, and that was what mattered. He was lucky too that the arrows sent into the air missed him completely, though from the cries below he knew the arrows had not missed everything though but had just found other targets.
And as the sun rose over the far tree line Ashley Pickles joined friends unmet and began the defense of the Great Thicket.

The Messy of old was gone, long gone, and in her place was the Queen of the Kingdom of Man and a full Mistress of Magic. When she had reached the hill she had suddenly been filled with a feeling of intense warmth as she ran up the rest of the hill and embraced the old man and felt tears and laughter fill her and before her was the Thicket, the place of so many whispers and tales.

"So this is it? This is why we are here?"

The man nodded, releasing her and turned to look at the great mass that made up the Thicket.

"All for this, yes. It has always been about this place, for much of our Kingdom. People who are afraid, who are desperate, who are empty, look for something to blame and for the people of our Kingdom, of many Kingdoms really, it is this place, it is the Great Thicket."

"And are, are they right to fear it"? Messy asked.

"Yes, as we are right to fear all things that are powerful, are magical, and are mysterious. But fearing a thing and hating it must not be the same. It is healthy to fear a thing so long as that fear does not win out, so long as it does not turn to hate, but as an apple left too long will rot, fear left too long will turn to hate. Especially when there is one such as Lady Hush to add fuel to that fear. If you are asking if there be monsters here, if there be monsters in the Great Thicket then Queen, I cannot tell you no. There be a great many thing, both dark and lovely, within the Thicket, but in knowing that there is both shadow and light within that unclaimed land I have to ask you - does it matter? Does it matter that great darkness lies within those woods? Darkness that would consume us all, if freed? Because with that darkness there is blinding light as well, to temper the dark and hold it back. As in all our hearts there is both darkness and light, so is it true here. So I ask again, does it matter?"

Messy took a moment to consider her words, knowing what she felt the answer was but wanting to understand *why* that answer was the right one. Finally –

"No, no it doesn't. Whatever lives within those woods is not our concern for now, what is our concern is protecting it. We must always protect the things that cannot protect themselves, even if we do not understand or fear those things."

"You make your mother and the other Queens proud, Mistress. Very proud indeed. Ah, I see your friend is back with us."

Messy looked up and saw the Meep Sheep spinning in the air above the people, uncertain it seemed who to go to among all those unhappy people in hopes of cheering them but as Messy watched an arrow erupted from the center of the mass and struck the sheep in the side. Messy screamed out and could only watch as the sheep flew for another brief moment then fell several feet to the ground. There was a terrible moment of silence before it regained the air and flew slowly up the hill, making it only as far as the base of the hill before it fell in a heap. Messy ran down the hill after it and was struck by a wave of heat that rose from bonfire and the people. She could hear their screams and above them the screams of Lady Hush, who was in a frenzy. When Messy reached the sheep she saw that it was still flapping its delicate wings in hopes of gaining the air but it couldn't manage it, the pain too great and the arrow too deep. She bent and gathered it up in her arms and turned her back on the crowd and started walking quickly up the hill again. First one, then another rock struck her from behind and she spun around to see arms frozen before they could throw their rocks, frozen by a look she gave them of pure hatred. How could these people be *her* people? How could they be the same people her mother had loved so dearly? She bit her tongue at the calls of witch that rang out but she turned back to the hill and walked the rest of the way without any more trouble. Once she crested the hill she laid the Meep Sheep onto the ground and knelt beside it. It lay panting before her, its legs kicking back and forth as it tried to right itself.

"What, what have they done?"

"Only what all frightened people do, dear Queen. They turned to violence to purge their fear. But we have other business. Now, let me see here, oh dear, yes, this is not good at all. No, no good at all." No One bent and inspected the sheep and shook his head as he did. Messy's heart broke.

"What, what is it? Will it be OK? Is, is it…"

"Good Queen, your Meep Sheep has an arrow in it. That is no good. No good at all. Why ever would someone store an arrow in a Meep Sheep?"
Messy was shocked at this attempt at humor as her friend was dying before her, the light in its eyes dimming slowly. No One looked over at Messy and saw her grief and, seeing this, knew that time was short. He reached down with one hand and held the sheep as he took the arrow in his other hand and pulled it out before Messy could stop him. The sheep yelped as he pulled the arrow out but there was no blood. No One then reached into a pouch he wore on his side and pulled out a small flask and poured a thick blue fluid over the wound. Again, the sheep yelped but as soon as he did this he let go of the sheep and in a moment it was up again and waddled over to butt its head against the Queen's. Messy could say nothing, could do nothing, she was in such deep shock but as the Meep Sheep rubbed against her face she couldn't help but giggle.

"Some things, my Queen, are not nearly as dire as they appear. You forget, I think, that you made the Meep Sheep yourself, and that something as simple as an arrow forged by man can do it no harm. Magic can cure many ills but what ills it cannot, belief and hope can cure. Now, our friend down the hill, who

comes yonder, his Bumble Kitty friends would not be as lucky should an arrow come their way but for your sheepie here, he is made of stronger stuff, and so are you."
Messy squeezed the Meep Sheep tight and it let out a 'meep' and she rose again and looked down the hill. There was trouble down near the fire, and as she watched a young man was raised up and the crowd began moving him towards the fire. Messy moved to run down to help but was stopped by No One.

"You made your own way here, Queen, let the boy make his own way. Things will be what they must be. All is not lost though, not lost by half, just look to the sky there, it seems he has friends as well."

And No One was right, just as all seemed lost the crowd stopped moving and slowly they released their grip on him and as she watched three Bumble Kitties came into view. The young man reached up and grabbed onto the kitties and they brought him quickly up the hill and to where she now stood. He wore dirty brown corduroy pants and a flannel shirt and was barefoot. His face was covered in soot but as dirty and miserable as he may have looked, it was a smile that greeted Messy but it was she that spoke first.

"Hello Ashley, I'm glad you made it."

"So am I Queen, so am I. And you must be No One, I think we spoke in my dreams, if I am not mistaken."

This time it was No One that laughed.

"After today you'll both be quite glad to have dreams free and clear of me and that awful Lady Hush I would bet. I am sorry for my part in them but that but it was the only way I could speak to you both and to lead you here. I knew that you both traveled dangerous roads and that you had someone, something, pulling you toward the shadows and wanted to be a light to guide you here. I hope I was some help."

Messy leaned over and kissed his cheek.

"You were more than just a light, my friend, more than just that and I am lucky for it. Now, where do we begin?"

"We begin with breakfast and a talk, and we go from there. They are coming, our friends down the hill, but not yet. Lady Hush has them, but she has some work to do to get them ready for war, to get them ready to kill. Perhaps noon will stir them to action but that is many hours away and I have some porridge on and you both look like you could use a warm meal. We can talk then."

Messy and Ashley followed No One into his small cottage and listened to him tell them the story of how it was he came by the recipe for the porridge they were about to eat. That story lead to another, to another, and another and it was clear that No One had not had anyone to speak to but the Great Thicket and the passing animals for a great many year. As much as they enjoyed the stories, it was hard to see how they prepared them for what seemed to be a war, and after several hours, when noon was at hand, it was Ash that finally broke in.

"No One, your stories are amazing, like songs in their own right but how will this stop the people at the bottom of your hill? How will this stop the fires?"

"Oh, well, oh. That was what you were waiting for all this time? That's why you let me ramble on for so long? Well aren't you two the sweetest young…well, to answer your question I have as much of an idea how to stop them as you do. I do however have a friend I have yet to ask the aid of though. Come, follow me."

No One lead Ash and Messy outside again and they all laughed to see the Bumble Kitties chasing the Meep Sheep around in circles, and every time the sheep would get ahead of them the third kitty one would flutter into the air and land on its back and ride the sheep for a moment. As soon as the kitty was on its back the sheep would stop in its tracks, turn, and chase the other kitties around. It was terribly distracting but worse was how large the fire was down the hill, and it was clear that the people were getting ready for their attack. Weapons had been brought forward, as had torches and all along the plain there were people, thousands and thousands of people, all gathered here to bring back the darkness to the world, whether they meant to or not. No One moved quickly to the edge of the Thicket and spoke to it in a soft voice.

"You have seen what folly lies down below, and you know what I and my friends are prepared to do, but what else do you see?"

"No One, you never ask the questions that you mean. I see far and wide. I see all that is and was. I see three against thousands. I see an old enemy of mine, an enemy of the Thicket that believes she can tame the darkness within, something I know she cannot. You ask me what I see and I tell you that I see hope against fire."

"And you are ever cryptic, O Thicket, so answer me what I ask – what do you *see*? And what should we *do*?"

There was a moment of silence before the voice came again from the Thicket, as if the entirety of the woods themselves were speaking.

"I see hope. I see help. And I see three souls with more power in their hope and in their abilities than any army might stop. It is to you, No One, one last task and then you are done. Then you can finally see what your fate holds. Can you do this one last thing?"

This time it was No One who considered his words carefully before he spoke.

"I am scared, but I am ready." He nodded to himself then and turned to face Messy and Ashley.

"I know what we shall do."

"What is that, No One?" Messy asked.

"We will do what we must."

No One took up his Sighing Pipe and walked to the crest of the hill and looked down at the people lined up against them down below. He saw behind their rage and into their hearts and it was hard, hard to see that much confusion. And who had stirred them? Was it Lady Hush alone, or had their own fear lead them to hatred and thus to this place and this day? Maybe it didn't matter in the end, maybe all that mattered was that they were here, all of them, and they were ready to die for an idea that was only half-formed.

Ashley stepped forward and took his place beside No One and took a deep breath to calm himself. His mother and father, and his village and his lost friend were all so far away, as if in another life altogether, yet they were here with him just the same, hidden in his heart but there. His hands ached and he missed his guitar more than ever but without it he had found that there was still just as much music in him as there ever was, he just had to find different ways to send that music into the world. He may never play guitar again, let alone many other things, as bad as his hands were, but the music was there, as it had been in that field of Umpton, waiting to get free, burning to get free, and he was ready to loose it on everyone down below.

Messy was the last to step forward, and she was the one most uncertain of herself, but that passed as it had in the dead grove with the Kreep Sheep. She was the Queen, and it was as simple as that. These were her people, and she loved them, all of them, even as she feared them. Messy was still unsure what she would do as she lined up with Ashley and No One but suddenly she was struck with a notion, and that was all it took.

Messy was the first to act of the three of them and she opened her arms wide, as if to embrace all the people that stood watching below, and as she did it she closed her eyes and set an image in mind and concentrated on it, and as she concentrated the sun started to dim until it was gone and in its place was the moon, and then nothingness. She brought the darkness. She opened her eyes and smiled. There were screams from below lead by Lady Hush and many of the people began throwing rocks that came nowhere near the three of them. Next it was No One's turn and he began to play the Sighing Pipe and with that raised the winds to carry the tune down the hill and to the people. Ashley joined him and caught the melody of his pipe and spun it into a song that rose to his mind as easily as if it had been there all along. As soon as Ash started singing the three kitties stopped their pursuit of the sheep and bounded forward and started purring in tune so that music filled the valley and fell like soft snow. For their part the people seemed to take notice and stop everything until, as before, the only sound that remained came from Lady Hush, who raged at the mob. The people remained silent and still as the song rang through the sudden night.

But that stillness did not last.

A whisper rose among the people and Lady Hush's black words were a quick poison that spread through everyone and roused them from their stupor. The people took up the fire and began to march forward.

Ash and No One concentrated and pushed the song harder, and the Thicket blew the wind harder but it was no good, as the people marched on, setting the brush and surrounding woods on fire and suddenly the woods Messy had traveled through became a grim inferno. The fire began to spread so fast that it would make escape nearly impossible and if Lady Hush had her way, no one would escape this valley.

Messy closed her eyes again and concentrated and suddenly the night was filled with lightning and thunder, but the people came on, and with them came the fire and the arrows and rocks, which were getting perilously close.

As the people grew closer and Lady Hush louder, hope returned, this time from the sky.

A great shadow that was darker than the gloom she had created spread over the expanse of the valley and Messy knew those shapes in a moment and a dozen War Pandas of the Panda Kingdom landed so that they encircled the fire and the people who bore it forward. One errant panda flew further on and landed behind Messy and her friends, its color radiating a deep red, the color of war for the War Panda, and a color of danger for all that stood in its way. Atop the Panda was Manda, the journalist Messy had left in that Kingdom to watch over things there. With her was an older panda that wore a wooden crown and held a small glowing globe between its paws. The War Panda, which towered over even the cottage and was half as tall as the great old trees of the Thicket, knelt so that Manda and the Great Loof could get off and once down. As soon as she was down Manda ran to her Queen.

"I am sorry we took so long to get here, the Great Loof wanted to make sure he had enough Pandas to aid you."

"But how did you know? How did you know we needed you?"

"Your councilors knew. Your Carriage had something in place to track it and when you abandoned it they came looking for you and it didn't take long for them to connect the talk of unrest and rumors that there was a woman who was raising an army to burn the Thicket. Anyway, we're here now and we're ready to fight with you."

Amanda smiled at her Queen and put up her fists as if ready to box her.

Loof stepped forward and Messy turned to him and bowed, and as she bowed, so did he and their foreheads touched and she giggled at how soft he was.

"It is time we took up arms with you my Queen. We have stood by and watched things play out for too long. Once we stood against you but now it is time we quelled this tide before it becomes a flood, but first, to put out that fire. It is time to stand together."

Loof stepped forward and held the globe in his hands aloft and blew in it and as he did it glowed from yellow to blue and he shook it fiercely and as he did a thick, heavy snow began to fall. Seeing the Pandas the people stopped, uncertain what to do next and frightened at seeing War Pandas, which were said to never have lost a battle, but as soon as they stopped the whisper rose again from Lady Hush and they moved forward once more. As the people moved forward the pandas in unison let out a roar that shook the valley and moved forward themselves toward the people. Screams of terror rang out and that terror was stronger than the prodding of Lady Hush and the people began running away from the Pandas. All along the valley the snow had begun to fall harder and bit by bit it began killing the fires.

Lady Hush howled with rage and ran to the forward of the people, demanding they stop. Her rage was such that her voice drowned out all other sound in the valley and she called up the hill.

"Enough games witch! You cannot stop us forever. If we fail today there will come another day when the whispers of unrest will return and if you stop us again we will rise another day but one day *promise you* there will come a fire that shall purify this land and there is nothing you can do to stop it. NOTHING!"

All eyes on the hill fell to Messy, who set her jaw and stepped forward.

"Know this, all of you – whatever you believe, whatever you whisper, and whatever you do, I will love you. No matter what. I will love you because I am your Queen. Hear me well, all of you – *I am your Queen!* I will suffer your insults and I will suffer your ignorance but I will *never* suffer you harming anyone or anything of this Kingdom or any other. All who rise against this Kingdom and its people will answer to me. All who betray this Kingdom have two options – to leave and never return or to face the wrath of the Great Thicket."

Lady Hush ran up the hill ahead of the people and hissed at Messy, taking up a rock and throwing it weakly at her. Loof, enraged at such insolence, charged down the hill at her and scared her back into the rest of the people, who also retreated from him. Messy raised her hand to stop him and she spoke again.

"*Enough!* I have had enough of this. Come with your fire if you mean to do it, come and we will stop you, otherwise go home, go home to your lives, go home and make this the Kingdom you wish it to be and stop blaming the Thicket and others for what you have not. You can join with me, with *us* and make this the Kingdom we all want, all deserve, or you can follow the fools and liars like Lady Hush and be consumed by the very fire you wish to spread. Whatever you choose, know only that I will love you, no matter what, and that I will do everything in my power to make this a place of serenity, peace, and joy again, but what happens next is up to you. *Make – Your – Choice!*"

With that Messy stepped back and with a wave of her arm she brought back the sun. The snow had put the fires out completely, both the bonfire and the fires in the trees so it was safe to bring back the sun and Messy was tired of the games. Was tired of using her magic, magic she had never known she had before this day, to frighten people she wished only to help. She was tired, she was sore, and she felt embarrassed to have let her anger get the better of her. Loof came and placed a paw on her shoulder.

"They are fools to have thought you weak, my Queen. Just as they would be fools to defy you. Any ruler can rule with anger, but it takes a great ruler to lead with love."

Messy leaned into the great Panda and hugged him, hoping he wouldn't feel the tears as they came to her eyes. Behind her, No One and Ashley had taken up their song again and as they did, by some strange magic not of Messy's making, she heard voices joining in. She spun around and yes, down in the valley the War Pandas, save one near the back of the crowd, had backed off and had gathered together near the base of the hill and all along the field people were joining together and singing. Not all of the people sang though as some were running off into the hills, back to their homes, or to their own Kingdoms. Messy was shocked though, shocked and amazed to see how many stayed, stayed to sing together, to join together, and to start cleaning up the mess they had made. People began gathering the detritus of their abandoned war and were piling it high where the bonfire had been as the wounded amongst them were tended to by others. Lady Hush, seeing that she had lost the day, ran, her back straight, her stride long and her face drawn into a snarl. As she was almost free of the valley and to the river where she could conjure a boat and escape the War Panda that had remained toward the back of the crowd snatched her up easily and gobbled her up before anyone could see. It hummed a little as she went down, the old woman tickling him with her anger, but after that tickle there was nothing and

Lady Hush was no more.

Atop the hill Manda joined Messy and Loof and the three of them simply stood and watched as the people sang and cleaned up the remnants of the war that never was. In the sky the three Bumble Kitties buzzed around their new friend the Meep Sheep and sang their song to the people below. It was not long before the one Meep Sheep was joined by another, then another, and another, another and *they* were joined by more Bumble Kitties and suddenly the sky was full of flying fluffy creatures that looked as if they had come from a dream. Manda gasped and Messy turned and behind the group of them came two Bloo Moos, wandering slowly from the Thicket as if it was nothing unusual.
No One laughed.

"My old friends, you've come back after these many years. It's good to see you."

Then the Thicket spoke.

"No One, it is time. It is time to come home."

All eyes were on No One then and the song died out on the hill, though it lived and thrived down in the valley. No One looked around at his friends, all of them new to him but seeming as if he had known them forever but it was time to finally discover the last of the old mysteries. It was time to see what truly lay beyond the Thicket.

"So, so you mean to go then? You mean to go and never return?" Asked Messy her eyes suddenly filled with tears.

"Oh, dear Queen, I have been here these great many years watching the Thicket, protecting it, spreading stories about it to scare off people who might try to harm the place, and all these years I have but stepped within that place once, for a moment, to save another Queen who was ailing. This is the last great mystery, if for no one else then for me, and I have been waiting for the day I might discover the world that lay beyond. It is time for me to go. It is time for me to pass the Sighing Pipe to another that will take my post."

No One looked at Ashley.

"Me?"

"It was always you, my friend. Always. You just had to discover the power in yourself that would allow you to take this task and take it willingly. The most powerful weapon you can ever wield in protecting the Thicket is music, and my friend, there have been few with more music in their souls than you have. I give you my Sighing Pipe, my cottage, my land, and all that I own, if you will take on this duty."

"And if you take it Ashley know that so long as I rule, and long after you will never be lonely. I am sorry No One was left alone so long, but it will never happen again. Never."

"No way, right Great Loof? He has lots of friends now." Manda piped up and Loof nodded his big head.

"Any friend of the Thicket is a friend to the Pandas. We have had an alliance for ages with the Thicket and those beyond its borders and have fought more than one war on its account."

And then there was silence as in the valley the songs went on. Each of them searched for more to say but sometimes words simply got in the way of the actions that meant so much more, so each in turn went to No One and hugged him and wished him all the best. Last was Ash, who was handed the Sighing Pipe as he was clapped on the back. No One leaned in and whispered to Ash then, whose eyes grew wide, and when No One pulled away Ashley nodded to him and nothing more was said between them. And with that, No One walked to the secret entrance he had always kept watch over and slipped through it and into the Great Thicket. And there are stories of the adventures No One had, and of the things he saw and did, but what those tales are, few know and fewer ever shall.

Messy, Manda, and Ashley gathered together and looked down into the valley. There was debris everywhere and while there were many hands, and even Panda paws, cleaning things up, it would take a lot of work to get it all picked up. The three of them looked at one another and nodded to each other and started walking down to join in. Behind them Loof and the War Panda started speaking to the Thicket and their laughter shook the woods and the ground alike. Three Bumble Kitties and a Meep Sheep dropped from the sky and landed in front of the three friends and chased one another down the hill as they joined the people, who laughed and laughed and laughed to see such silliness after what had come before and joining that laughter was Messy, Ashley, and Manda, who were welcomed with open arms and open hearts.

The dawn had broken through what had seemed like an endless night. Oh, the night would come, but the lanterns of friendship would be lit against it and, with hope, the dawn would always come.
Always.

And while there are few happily ever afters, there can always be happy endings.

butter bug

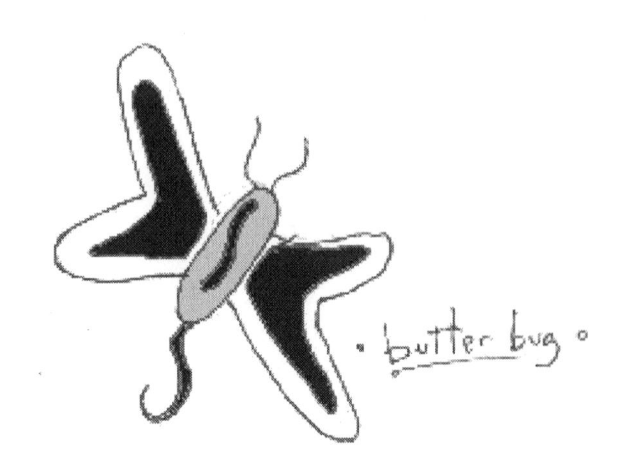
butter bug

Farewell

Amanda wiped away the tears as her automated carriage left the city of the Pandas and headed her into the snow and to a home she hadn't been to in ages. She had been with the Pandas serving the Queen for two years and in that time she had made friendships such as she had never had before. Much had changed since the first time she had come here in the hopes of bringing snow back to her home on Festival Eve. Had it not been for her family and boyfriend waiting for her she would be tempted to stay with the Pandas forever but there were other adventures, and other stories for her to write and it was time for Manda to return to her life. It was time to go back home and back to writing stories that didn't involve the wonderfully complex world of the Pandas. The Kingdom of Man was in a new age of prosperity and there were new wonders it seemed every day. Since Queen Messy had become Queen and Mistress of Magic she had worked hard to build friendships with the neighboring Kingdoms and had begun relations with the Great Thicket, and all the while she had encouraged and shepherded a new age of the Arts. Manda was to start covering the Outer Realm, perhaps even venturing into the neighboring Kingdoms to start seeing how they live, so it was time to leave her friends and head home.

A sob escaped Manda as she looked out the back window of the carriage and saw her friend Kindri, a young assistant to the elders, her friend Alloos with the younger Panda and both waving goodbye. There had been a grand ball the night before in her honor, not so much a 'goodbye' as a 'fare well', and it had been something she would always cherish, especially the many dances she had with the Pandas on hand. .

"Goodbye is for war, Miss Manda...and for the dead. You are going to neither, so this is fare well." She was told gruffly, though there were tears in the voice of Ruuuj, one of the honor guards in the city who had been one of the last to warm to her but who had become one of her closest friends.

Yes, not goodbye, just fare well.

Amanda forced herself to look away from Kindri and turned around to face forward and look toward the road ahead, which was covered over with the winter snow. Behind her the preparations were already being undertaken for the Renewal Festival, which they had taken to celebrating regularly again. Amanda had been a big part of the Pandas having Renewal Festivals again, and the Pandas would always love her for that. No one had anticipated how well the Pandas would take to her, especially not Manda herself, but it was true, and the Kingdom had changed because of this friendship. In fact, were it not for her, what began as unrest in the Outer Realm may have become full war if Zoof, one of the Panda elders, had not gone to speak with the people and taken the Winter globe with him, and it was that which turned the tide. The wonderment that could be created with that magic globe was enough to calm the tide of that budding war and so this would be another season of peace for the Kingdom of Man. Manda smiled thinking this and it was that warmth that took the tears away.

The snow was a blur outside the small window as the carriage picked up speed and Manda looked down at the small green box she held in her hands, a final gift from her friend and grand elder of the Pandas, Loof. He had told her, the day before she was leaving, that he preferred to see her off then, so it was not truly anything more than a fare well, because she had not departed yet. In sending her off though, he gave her the one gift she accepted from the Pandas - a small green box. It was not that she didn't desire to take the beautiful presents that were offered her but she knew their culture well and that gifts were only accepted like that by the family of someone who has passed away, and she was clearly not departing anything more than this land for another. So what she did was have the Pandas leave the many gifts of food, clothing, and the beautiful sculptures that were part of their heritage with Alloos, who kept a small cottage for Amanda, should she return. It was a nice thought for her, a warm thought that there was a place for her there. There was a home.

Ah, but when she'd ever get to return was the

question.

Much had changed in her time with the Pandas and there was much to report, and Manda was still the lead reporter for the Kingdom and as such, wherever there was something important, she was there. So when she might return she wasn't sure, but she would.

Some day.

She hoped.

Ah, but the box.

The snow was a blur beyond the window and the sun was fading. It would still be hours until she was home again and that was an awful long time to think so the box was the perfect distraction. The box was small and green and though simple at first glance, was very ornate. Small, stones had been woven into the fabric, and though they were nothing valuable, their rarity to the Pandas and in their lands made them of great value to Amanda. Tears started to run down her face again.

She wasn't sure what she expected to be in the box but part of her didn't want to know. Opening the box would take away the last mystery she had left from the place. Maybe the last she would ever have from there.

More tears.

But then, deep in her mind, she heard the voice of Loof, who had once told her that as long as there were sunrises, there were mysteries. Mysteries did not pass with the person - they only became greater, broader, and more wondrous. Each day, he concluded, is a new world, a new mystery, a new life – it is for us to link these days together or to push into the thickets and make a new path.

Manda nodded to herself.

To not open the box would be an insult. She must be brave, she must be bold.

She must forge ahead.

Amanda took a deep breath and opened the box.

Within the small green box was a red key atop dozens of coins of different color, size, and seemingly denomination. Even in the dim light of the carriage the key sparkled atop the coins and she couldn't help but smile. Fastened to the inside of the lid of the box was a note, which Amanda pulled out to read.

Miss Manda – I give to you my most cherished treasure – a Key of Dreams. I was given this by a shaman from a lost Tribe of Man many, many years before our histories were recorded. I give this now to you, you who have bridged the Panda Kingdom with the Kingdom of Man once more. I give this to you and smile, knowing the adventures I had with this key when I was younger and had far more dance in my paws. This key is for not a door but for an idea, for a dream; and dreams, my dear, can be found everywhere one looks. When a day comes when you need an escape, when you need an adventure, when you need a new story to tell then take this little red key, close your eyes, and think of where you want to be. When you have that in mind, hold the key out and turn it and a door shall appear and through that door you will arrive wherever it was you dreamed. To return, you do the same. This key is as magical or terrifying as the user wishes, so be warned not to dream darkly unless you wish to see the shade. Use it well, and I trust, some day, you will use this key to dream of us, so we might see you once again.

Amanda couldn't stop the tears as they coursed down her face, nor could she stop the smile that lit her up and warmed her as they were linked. She lifted the key and it was light, light but warm, and she smiled more broadly, a place in mind, a person in mind, and closed her eyes and held the key out and turned it and felt a lock click open and then a breeze. She wondered a moment about her luggage and then laughed – the carriage would go to wherever it was bidden to travel, with our without its passenger. She took a deep breath and leaned forward, eyes still closed, and fell into nothingness, and into the waiting arms of the one she loved.

And somewhere, far, far away, a grand old Panda laughed, as if tickled by a breeze or by the kiss of someone precious, and it was a smile that lit its face as it fell back into slumber.

meepus sheepus

bloo moo

bumble kitty

~ THANK YOU ~

This is one of those things where I could literally thank hundreds of people but really don't have the space. I owe a great debt of gratitude to everyone who has inspired, encouraged, read, and loved me, and none of this is possible without these people. You are always bound to 'leave people out' and it is a shame but, for me, I would rather send it out to everyone rather than point out a few people. This book was another one that was never meant to become this, though I am glad it did. I had a notion, years and years ago, about little flying sheepies that could make people happy if you hugged them. What came with them were small little kitties that flew around on bee wings (ah, how things change). I didn't know quite what to do with these critters until two friendships inspired me to make these critters more substantial. First came *Messy and the Meep Sheep* and when that was done I felt compelled to give the Bumble Kitties a home and so next came *Ashley Pickles and the Bumble Kitties.* It wasn't until I met one more person, a person who stole my heart fair and square that I had a third person and critter to add to the mix. This is where *Manda and the Pandas* came in, and after that story, well, I had to even it all out.

See, this was meant to be a book, a small book, and maybe a second, but as the stories compiled it became clear that this was a bigger project than I had anticipated. When I put This Beautiful Darkness together I had in mind that the next book to come down the chute would be the one you now hold. I had wanted to do a full edition with lots of art and all but, well, waiting for the artists to appear, or for my skill to come to a point where I felt it was complimentary was not going to happen any time soon so I had to just put this together. I love these stories dearly and hope you will also.

I owe so much to people but all I can do is say *thank you.*

Thank you to *Messy Stench* for being the inspiration and template for our young Queen Messy.

Thank you to *Ashley Peacock* for being the inspiration for Ashley Pickles

Thank you, thank you to *Amanda Emery* for inspiring Manda and for supporting and encouraging me at every step.

Thank you to my friends, my family, my co-workers, to the artists who inspire me, to the people who reviewed me, to the people who podcasted me, and to everyone who I meet and met at art shows and conventions. I write because I love it, I publish because I love you.

I hope you enjoy the journey through the Kingdom of Man as much as I enjoyed bringing it to you.

And always remember - magic takes time.

– Chris Arrrr - 2010

Layout by ***Amanda Emery***
All words and images and cover by ***Chris Ringler***
Font and additional cover work by ***Marcus Bieth***
Editing assistance from ***William Evans***

Lord Chris of Ringler was born in Flint, Michigan and raised in the nearby village of Linden, where he was taught the way of the blade at an early age. Having thwarted all his enemies at age five, Young Lord Ringler went on to Master the great arts of the world, growing bored with his mastery at age eight. The burden of greatness weighing heavily upon him, Lord Ringler ran away from the life of luxury he was accustomed to train in the art of Circus Clownery. It was here that he fell in love again with the arts and writing. Lord Ringler returned from a long absence to publish his first book Back From Nothing. During a renowned book tour that lasted ten years Lord Ringler was published in BARE BONE and CTHULHU SEX MAGAZINE. He has also received Honorable Mention in THE YEAR'S BEST FANTASY AND HORROR twice. Lord Ringler graced the world with his second book, This Beautiful Darkness, in 2009 and it has been an international best seller never. In his scant free time Lord Ringler paints, takes photos, draws, and re-writes classic works of literature and music to make them more gooder. He is not a robot.

Set browsers to RINGLER for more info on the legend that is Chris Ringler. You will not be disappointed.
Yet.

Also by ***Chris Ringler***

- Back From Nothing
- This Beautiful Darkness

Smoochapotamus

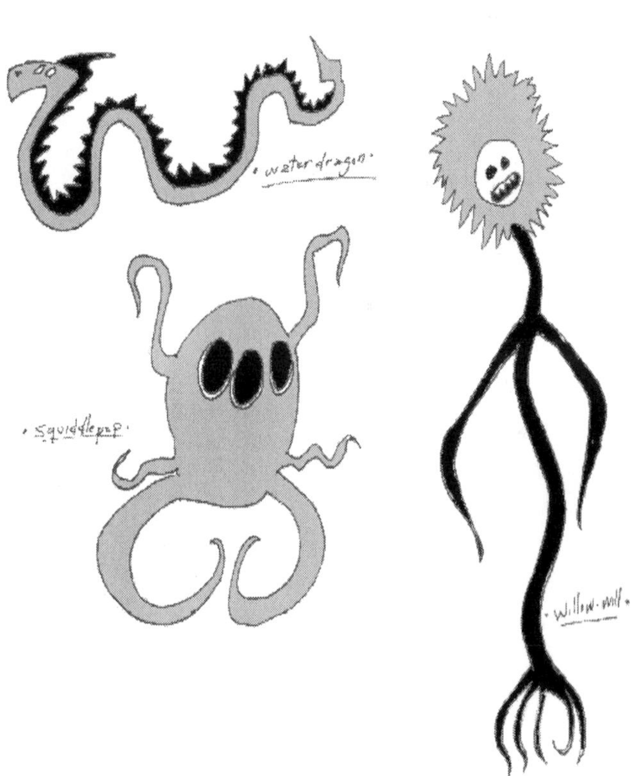
water dragon
Squiddlepup

Made in the USA
Charleston, SC
10 April 2014